I0645882

Escape from Heaven

Pulpless.Com™ Books by J. Neil Schulman

Novels
Alongside Night
The Rainbow Cadenza
Escape from Heaven
Raising Hell (forthcoming)

For Children and Young Adults
The Wish-Me Well (forthcoming)
Santa Honica (forthcoming)
Tick-Tock, The Man in the Clock (forthcoming)

Nonfiction
The Robert Heinlein Interview and Other Heinleiniana
The Frame of the Century?
Stopping Power: Why 70 Million Americans Own Guns
Book Publishing in the 21st Century, Volumes One and Two

Short Stories
Nasty, Brutish, and Short Stories

Omnibus Collections
Self Control Not Gun Control
Gefilte Ham (forthcoming)

Collected Screenwritings
Profile in Silver and Other Screenwritings

Escape from Heaven

A novel by

J. Neil Schulman

PULPLESS.com
A Division of Duj Pepperman Enterprises
150 S. Highway 160, Suite C8, #234
Pahrump, NV 89048
Voice: (310) 839-7653
Fax: (801) 904-7851
eMail: info@pulpless.com
Home Page: http://www.pulpless.com/

PULPLESS.com™

Copyright © 2002 by J. Neil Schulman
All rights reserved. Published by arrangement with the author. Printed in the United States of America. The rights to all previously published materials by J. Neil Schulman are owned by the author, and are claimed both under existing copyright laws and natural logorights. All other materials taken from published sources without specific permission are either in the public domain or are quoted and/or excerpted under the Fair Use Doctrine. Except for attributed quotations embedded in critical articles or reviews, no part of this book may be reproduced or utilized in any form or by any means, electronic or mechanical, including photocopying, recording, or by any information storage and retrieval system, without written permission from the publisher.

This novel is fiction. Names, characters, places, and incidents either are products of the author's imagination or are used fictitiously. Any resemblance to actual events, locales, or persons, living, dead, or immortal, is entirely coincidental.

First Edition
Library of Congress Catalog Card Number: 2001097315
Hard Cover ISBN: 1-58445-192-0
Trade Paperback ISBN: 1-58445-189-0

Book designed by *e*and*i*Publishing.com
Cover by Billy Tackett, Arcadia Studios
© 2002 by Billy Tackett

To My Father Who Art In Heaven
And To My Family Who Art On Earth

A Revelation

Everything is different than I thought.
What I thought was my cage
was the nest I'd built for myself.
What I thought was my life
was just my basic training.

We really don't know what's going on
right next to us.
The universe is so strange,
so surprising,
so dramatic.

Life can be exactly like
the most exciting novel
and for the writer,
how could I not jump in
to play one of the roles?

Shakespeare, after all,
used to play his characters.

But it's different
when your character suddenly is *You*,
and you find out
that you're not what you thought you were.

What had just been glimpses
through a dark glass
before
became an open window
for a few hours.

Do you know how long a few hours is
and what you can see
if you look around?
I wanted a glimpse
my curiosity was boundless
and be careful what you pray for
because the guy who answers
"Thy will be done"
has a real rough sense of humor.

The thing is, he climbed inside with me
and let me share the joke.

Unbefuckingleivable.

The game's afoot!
Heinlein was right.
Yoda was right.

The universe is not what it seems
and,
the amazing thing is

Neither are You.

February 18, 1997

Part 1
A Call from God

Chapter One

There's an old saying that everybody wants to go to Heaven but nobody wants to die.

That's how it was for me, anyway.

I drove a Mercedes because I was told it was the safest car in a crash. And it was a smart choice. I died of something else.

I owned a handgun so I wouldn't die at the hands of a burglar. I was right about that, too. The burglar who broke into my bedroom ran like hell when he saw the .45 Government Model I was pointing at him ... and I died of something else.

I quit smoking, did my best to keep my weight down and eat a low cholesterol diet, and practiced safe sex, because I didn't want to die of cancer, heart disease, emphysema or AIDS, and it paid off: I died of something else.

You see, that's the part they forget to mention. No matter what nasty ways of dying you avoid, there's always another one waiting for you. If one thing doesn't get you, another thing will. Everybody could have saved a lot of thought that went into bumper stickers and public service messages. All they would have had to say is, "Don't do that. Die of something else."

It would have saved me a lot of trouble, too. I was a coward most of my life because I was afraid of dying.

My story begins the day I died and went to Heaven.

It was a slow news day. Here in Los Angeles, no riots, no brushfires, no mudslides, no earthquakes, no celebrities being accused of child molesting, hit and run, wife-beating, trafficking in drugs, or murder. On the national and international scene, no terrorist attacks, no school yard shootings, no one holed up in a church surrounded by the Feds, no movie idol or politico getting caught with a prostitute, no husband looking for his johnson in the traffic island, no custody battles with a communist dictator acting in loco parentis.

The sort of day that strikes fear into the hearts of talk radio hosts like me.

Okay, I'm exaggerating. A little. Some of the best shows have been on slow days. I once heard Tom Leykis when he was on KFI, do a spellbinding three-hour monologue — no calls, only commercial breaks — just telling how he got into this business. Phil Hendrie is the radio equivalent of fantasy mud wrestling. But if you don't have that sort of talent for improv — and I don't — then you succeed or fail by the quality of calls you get.

Talk radio topics get divided between the social issues and the personal issues — the macro and the micro, as my old friend Dennis Prager calls it. As a general rule, people are more willing to talk about the personal issues with women hosts who put the word "doctor" before their first name. There have been exceptions — David Viscott, for example — but that usually requires diplomas I didn't have. Other talk show hosts had no problem getting the phones filled with wives calling about their husband's cheating or gay men talking about their lovers dying of AIDS, but that wasn't the sort of listenership I tended to attract. My listeners wanted politics, current events, controversy. I wasn't pushing the outside of the outrageousness envelope, like Imus or Howard Stern. I was a pundit, a loudmouth. In other words, a Rush Limbaugh/Larry King wannabee, like almost everyone else in talk radio.

I could always get the phones lit up by talking about abortion, or gun control, or political correctness, or illegal immigration. But you don't want to hit on those too often. You just keep hearing the same arguments over and over, usually from the same callers. (And yes, I know it's you, even if you give my call screener a phony name and pretend you're on the other side so we put you on for the third time that month.)

There are certain subjects that will light up the board with callers you just don't want to go near. People who say they've been abducted by UFO's. Callers reincarnated from Marilyn Monroe — and not just women, either. People who say they've figured out the doughnut assassination, or claim they know where Bill Gates is. Mysterious deaths of pets owned by powerful politicians. Waco, 911 Tuesday revisionists, the International Space Station explosion, militias, endless conspiracy theories. Any of these calls you take, no matter how good your call screener, is walking through a minefield. And most of them are just unoriginal — bad radio. You really have to have the bizarre talents of an Art Bell to succeed in that sort of market.

I guess I was desperate. I was coming back from my first commercial break after the news, evening drive time and my second of four hours, Monday through Friday — and if you called me right now, you were not going to get a busy signal. A bad situation.

My engineer, Terry, had a cruel sense of humor. For the musical bump leading back into the show, I was hearing on my phones Frank Sinatra singing, "It's quarter to three, there's no one in the place …except you and me…" I gave Terry the finger and he grinned from the other side of a plate-glass window.

I hit the cough button to clear my throat and came in a half beat too late: "You're listening to 680 K-TALK, and I'm Duj 'Rhymes-with-Judge' Pepperman. The time is exactly 5:19. That little musical interlude is my engineer's not-so-subtle way of telling me I'm dying. So for the rest of the hour let's talk about death. The big D. Specifically, do you believe in life after death? Our number again is 1-888-55-K-TALK."

My producer, Jules, rolled her eyes heavenward. She was the one who was going to have to talk to all the assorted loose nuts who were about to call in. But it didn't take long for the video screen in front of me to start filling up with descriptions of new callers — and some of them were bound to be airworthy.

Okay, it was a cheap trick. You don't keep evening drive time in a top-rated market unless you do sheer entertainment once in a while.

My video screen said that line two had a 38-year-old woman who was having an affair with a ghost. I hit the private intercom to Jules, behind the glass. When the intercom button is pressed, my broadcast mike is cut off, allowing private conversations with my engineer or producer. "Line two," I said to Jules. "Calling from the Twilight Zone?"

Jules shook her head and gave me a hand signal that I interpreted as meaning "sex"; Jules didn't speak to me because she was screening another call.

I released the intercom and punched up line two. "Marie in Torrance," I said, "you're on K-TALK with Duj Pepperman."

"Duj? I can't believe I got through! I've been trying to call for weeks!"

I hit my intercom again and blew Terry a razzberry.

Releasing the intercom button again, I went back to my caller.

Marie's "ghost" sounded suspiciously to me like Patrick Swayze in the movie of that title, but I didn't say it. As long as she didn't get hotter than PG-13 in her description of her romantic relations with him, I could let her go on about him a bit. Nobody was going to be punching up KRLA.

Listening with one ear, I went back to reading through my fan mail (okay, hate mail, too) and wondered why anyone in my job ever wanted to move over to TV. Sure, the money was better, but with the camera on you all the time you had to work for it. And wear a suit. And get recognized in restaurants, too. I had a monthly audience averaging a few million, yet nobody ever asked me for an autograph while I was standing at a urinal. What celebrity can ask for more than that?

I thanked Marie for her call, went to a traffic report, told Terry to cart the new Purple Web commercial, then read it live while he recorded it for posterity, and returned to the live phones. My call monitor said line seven had "God" calling from "Paradise," and the subject was "Personal proof that life-after-death exists." I guessed that "God" was Jules' abbreviating Godfrey, and while Paradise, California is a few hundred miles north of our usual daytime broadcast area, we get calls from all over from satellite radio and our web cast. "Godfrey from Paradise," I said, "this is Duj Pepperman and you're on 680 K-TALK."

"Duj," said a rich baritone voice. A good radio voice. *My* voice. "This is God, calling from Heaven. I can't believe I got through. I'm one of your biggest fans!"

I immediately hit the "delete" button, but it didn't work and the call continued, "Listen, Duj, would you mind dying tonight and meeting tomorrow morning at my palace in Heaven? We need to talk privately."

I punched the intercom to Terry. "Kill line seven!" I hoped he could wipe the call before the four-second delay finished and the call went on the air.

There are words in life you never want to hear. A doctor pointing at an X-ray of your brain and saying "inoperable tumor." Calling your business manager's office and having a voice answer, "Frauds Detail, Detective Smith." Any call from your child's school that contains the word "accident."

The words that I heard next fell into that category. It was my engineer saying, "Kill what? There was no one on seven."

The primal part of me gasped. I looked at the display again. Now there was nothing on the monitor for line seven. The professional in me, trained never to allow long silences on the air, took over immediately, and before releasing the intercom I said, "Not funny, Terry!"

Terry looked innocent and shrugged.

Jules looked at me blankly, and shrugged, too. It was obvious that neither of them had any idea what I was talking about.

I didn't have time to worry about it now; the studio ON AIR light was still glowing.

I shrugged back. No reason to let my colleagues think I was losing it. "Modern technology strikes again," I said lamely, and punched up line eight. "Bob in Long Beach, you're on 680 K-TALK with Duj Pepperman."

It was only after the show was over that it crossed my mind that I might have been the first talk show host in human history to get a live call-in from God.

And I had hung up on Him.

There's something about having a few hundred thousand people listening to you that makes you feel invulnerable. Or maybe it's that the studio feels like a fortress — the fences and guard posts you have to pass to get in, the labyrinth-like corridors, the enforced quietude of the studio when the ON AIR light is lit.

Glitches happen all the time in radio. If it was a little strange to be hearing a voice my engineer couldn't and having a call disappear from the board, each had happened before. The only strange thing about it was both happening at the same time.

When I had a minute to think about it after I was off

the air, I decided it might be a high-tech prank of some sort — a computer virus maybe. I decided if it happened again, I'd let the station's management look into it.

The human mind is wonderful at not seeing the things it doesn't want to see. By the time I left the studio, I'd convinced myself everything was perfectly mundane. Usually you had to be that way, if you're going to get through the day. Just for example, you turned on the morning news and spent two seconds seriously wondering whether even a fraction of the terrible things you heard about could happen to you, you'd never have left the house. Not in L.A., anyway.

All things considered — as they say on the competition's show — it's amazing any of us got out of bed in the morning. Or could manage to fall asleep at night.

It's just a ten-minute drive from the K-TALK studios on Motor to my town home in Culver City. I drove into the complex through the main gate, past the empty guard shack. We used to spend a couple of thousand dollars per unit each year to keep a rotation of guards in that shack. It didn't stop a series of burglaries — and one rape — so there was a discussion at the Home Owners Association meeting. First, the board voted to demand the security firm to fire one guard, for sleeping on the job. Then a lot of ideas were batted around. One of the HOA's directors, an LAPD cop, came up with an idea that everybody laughed at until they realized he was serious. Then a few other people said, "What the hell, it couldn't hurt." The board passed a resolution, adopting it.

The next day, posted on the guard shack, was a paper target showing the outline of a man, courtesy of our cop-in-residence. The target is riddled with bullet holes — big ones. Nobody's been broken into since and we voted to get rid of the guards entirely.

When I got in I checked my phone messages and private email. The only message was a call from my ex-wife, the rock star, reminding me that the semester's USC tuition was due. Our daughter, Felony, wants to be the next Quentin Tarantino. Before you laugh at my daughter's given name, I have it on reliable authority that, nearing the end of Felony's freshman year, my 18-year-old daughter is still a virgin. I dialed my business manager's voice mail and played my ex's message into the cordless.

You might think that, being on radio, I never had to spend a night alone. You'd be wrong. The truth is, I just didn't get all that many opportunities to meet women. I didn't have a lot of guests on my show, so I was pretty well sitting alone in a glass-enclosed room four hours a day. Then I went home to an empty town home. I don't like parties or bars, I'm terrible with pick-up lines, and I think I'd have had better luck dating the first dozen single women in the phone book than the women I'd met through classified ads, the Internet, and dating services. I'd have had better luck meeting women if I'd been "recovering," but you had to be addicted to something, first. Take my word, it's not as easy for a radio talk-show host to get dates as it looked on *Frasier*.

I knew my freezer was full but I wasn't in the mood to defrost. I jumped back in my car and onto the Richard M. Nixon Freeway to Marina del Rey—all two miles of it. Fifteen minutes later I was chowing down on a tongue and Swiss cheese on rye at Jerry's Famous Deli.

That's where it happened. That's where I remembered that I was God.

Chapter Two

Did you ever find a million dollars that you forgot you had?

That's about as close as I can come in describing how I felt at that moment.

It's not that anything around me changed physically at the moment of revelation. I was still sitting at a table in Jerry's Famous Deli. My sandwich was still in front of me. So was my glass of Dr. Brown's celery tonic and a dish of pickles.

What was different is that I wasn't Duj Pepperman anymore.

I looked around the restaurant, at the other people. I saw them for a moment on the surface; then it was as if my vision went around a corner and I was seeing them from another angle, not just on the outside, but from the inside out, and with perspective both on their past and future.

I looked at a waiter and I knew that his fondest wish at the moment was to get the part he was up for on *General Hospital.*

A young woman sitting at the next table had just been told by her doctor that she was pregnant ... but not by her husband, who was sitting at the table next to her, and had no idea. She wanted to keep the baby. So would he ... but only if he thought it was his.

I looked over to a trim middle-aged man with a shaved head, sitting a few tables away, an ex-army colonel who had served with distinction in the Gulf

War. He had been forcibly retired due to a sexual ha-
rassment scandal involving men under his command,
but that he, personally, had nothing to do with. Now
he was middle management of a small computer software company and was about to be laid off, although
he didn't know it yet. His greatest wish was just one
more mission where he could make a difference.

Across from me, at another table, was a short curly-
haired man who had been a successful writer of science-fiction paperbacks—mostly media tie-ins. The
book contracts had dried up and he was now working
as a technical writer. He had completed an original,
science-fiction novel with an epic theme that he hoped
would be his break into hardcover publication and
serious reviews, but so far no one would touch it and
it was breaking his heart.

The TV over the bar had CNN on. A prominent U.S.
senator was being interviewed about a bill she had
introduced for a comprehensive national health plan.
She should have been focusing instead on her own
health; she was addicted to both amphetamines and
barbiturates that she used to mask the pain of her
husband's serial adultery. She had shut down sexu-
ally, converted her libido into power lust, and covered
it all with a smile that was permanently glued onto
her face.

I looked in the bar mirror, at myself.

I saw that my life until that moment had been prepa-
ration for this one, that "Duj Pepperman" was a ficti-
tious identity, that his life until that moment had been
a series of training exercises waiting for my arrival. I
felt that I'd just arrived after a long journey but regis-

tered surprise at how overweight this body was.

I laughed silently. Until that moment, Duj Pepperman had been an atheist.

There were two staggeringly beautiful women with elfin ears, both of them blond, almost albino, sitting a few tables away from me, looking at me intently. I recognized them as angels named Estella and Sophia. They recognized me as well. I nodded to them; they nodded back.

I paid my check and walked out to the parking lot. They were waiting for me in front of Sebrings hair stylists, where I had parked.

"I can't commit suicide," I told them. "I'm bound by the rules."

Estella nodded. "Don't worry, we understand our orders." She pulled a Glock 9-millimeter pistol from her jacket pocket and pointed it at me.

Sophia said, "Give me your keys."

I gave the keys to Sophia, who unlocked the doors with the remote. Estella opened the rear passenger door, motioning me in with the gun. I got into the back seat of my car, Estella following, with the gun still pointed at me. She reached across and pulled down the shoulder strap, buckling me in.

Sophia got behind the wheel of my car, started the ignition, and drove off, while Estella pulled a roll of duct tape out of her handbag. "Give me your hands," Estella said.

Holding the gun on me with one hand, she bound my hands to the seat belt, ripping the tape off with her teeth, then bound my feet. I tested the strength of the tape. She'd done a good job.

Sophia turned on the radio and tuned it to KLSX FM. The Beach Boys were singing "Good Vibrations."

Both angels started singing along, "I'm pickin' up good vibrations, she's giving me excitations ..."

Still singing, Sophia drove onto Admiralty Way. I started singing along with the angels, "Good, good, *good*, good vibrations!"

Sophia turned left on Via Marina, then onto a pier leading out to the harbor. Sophia accelerated the car while opening all four windows. The car leapt the pier and splashed. The Mercedes floated a few seconds then began sinking. Water began rushing in through the open windows.

"Na na na na na ... na na na!" sang Sophia, Estella, the Beach Boys, and me.

All of a sudden, the angels vanished and their voices cut off. Just as suddenly, I was no longer God.

The radio shorted out and went silent. I stopped singing, mid-vibration.

I was Duj Pepperman again, bound with duct tape into the back seat of a Mercedes that was sinking into cold salt water, water that was quickly rising up my chest.

"God, where did you go?" I shouted, panicked. "Why did you leave me?"

There was no answer.

I took a deep breath as the water rose toward my chin. Used all my strength to try to break the duct tape, but it was no use.

"Oh, shit!" I said, took one more breath, my last, then sunk beneath the water and drowned.

Chapter Three

If you'd seen anybody on TV telling you what it's like to die, the one thing you could pretty well be sure of is that they didn't die all the way. So you might have heard the beginning part about what happens when you die before ... but the part you'd heard was the part before it got really interesting.

Yes, I was outside of my drowning body almost immediately, floating about a dozen feet above the water. I could see things that I couldn't have seen if I'd had to rely on my old eyes. It was after dark, and the Mercedes had already sunk under the water far enough that all I should have been able to see of it was the roof and a few air bubbles rising to the surface of the water. But I could apparently see right through the solid roof of the car down to my tied-up waterlogged body.

My drowned corpse should have been a gruesome sight but the part of me that was capable of being disturbed was left behind with my old nervous system. I can be dispassionate now in trying to describe what the experience was like but being outside my body was an emotional rush at the time, and the second peak experience I'd had within an hour.

You've heard before, from people who've described their death experiences, about the bright light. That's part right and part wrong. We experience it as light, but it's not what a scientist of our time would have defined as light. It's not made up of photons (which you'd no longer have an optic nerve to perceive anyway), it's not an electromagnetic phenomenon at all, but we call it light because that's what we're perceiving.

I could stop this narrative right now and switch to writing a textbook about what we are when we are no longer living in flesh. The skeptical talk-show host I was a few hours earlier would have been interested in questions about how we could think without a brain or central nervous system to process information, how we can see without a retina to catch the photons, why we still feel without neural receptors to be compressed, and so forth. If you're really interested, you can do a search on astral physiology in the Tree of Knowledge, or just take a class. If you've read books on out-of-body and death experiences, keep in mind that about three-quarters of what you read was the guesswork of an author who, if he'd even reincarnated, was suffering from dinatal amnesia.

The short answer is: you're a burrito. You're an astral body stuffed into a flesh body. You have a consciousness that uses your brain like a computer mouse; you have a second body that is made out of a more durable substance than matter but can be hooked into flesh for a time. Your personality is not trapped in your brain but can be uplifted out of it; your fleshly body is designed for use in the plane of earth and once you're out of it for good, it's time to stick out your thumb, so to speak, and hitch a ride in the tunnels.

The light is, among other things, a boarding announcement.

I could see a tunnel mouth forming above me, and felt myself rising slowly at first. I hesitated, feeling an unbroken connection to my teenage daughter, but "remembered" being God again momentarily, and knew that I'd be seeing her again soon enough.

I allowed myself to be sucked up into the mouth and felt myself accelerating.

The tunnel was more like a glowing energy field than something made out of brick and mortar. If this was a movie, the special-effects shot of going into a tunnel would be like the *Millennium Falcon* going into hyperspace, or like the *Starship Enterprise* going into warp. And why not? The closest science came to describing a tunnel was a wormhole, and that's wildly inaccurate. It's a system of passageways that can be used for travel between worlds, universes, dimensions, time periods, and other sorts of places that twenty-first-century cosmology doesn't even encompass yet. The tunnel between earth and Heaven is like a local on the New York City subway, if you consider all the possible destinations. Heaven is about two million years in the future and five thousand degrees to the left. Practically walking distance.

When my daughter was little, we'd start singing "Ahhhhhhhhhhhh!" whenever we drove through a tunnel. I'm not sure why but I started singing "Ahhhhhhhhhhhh!" and decided to see how long I could keep it up. I soon noticed that there was another voice singing along with me. I, and whoever was joining me, didn't have to sing very long; I don't think I was in the tunnel for more than a minute before I popped out the other end.

I felt myself landing on my feet. There wasn't a mirror but I could look down and see that I seemed to have an ordinary body again, torso, arms and hands, legs and feet. Gravity—I could feel weight on my feet. Clothes, the same ones I'd been wearing when I left.

I looked around. My first impression of the arrival platform was aural rather than visual. I stopped singing "Ahhhhhhhhhhhh!" the moment I was out of the tunnel; but the other voice that had been singing along with me continued and was now close by. But I couldn't see anything yet. For my new eyes, the place was supersaturated with light and objects were hard to distinguish. I could see only light and shadows.

One of the shadows moved toward me. I made an effort to focus and the shadow resolved into a silhouette, and the figure resolved into a human form, and the human form resolved into a very pretty girl who looked to be about 12 years old. It took another beat before I recognized her. She had been 18 years old the last time I had seen her, two weeks earlier.

"Hi, Daddy," she said.

It was my daughter, Felony.

"Sweetie?" I said, shocked. "I don't understand. You were in college when I left earth. Was there an accident? Are you dead, too?"

She came up close and hugged me; she had to reach up the way she used to when she was little. "I'm fine, Daddy," she said. "I'm alive now and I'm alive back at college, when you left."

"I don't understand."

"Everybody who's going to end up here is already here," she said. "This is the end of time. This is

Heaven."

I looked around but the only thing that I could see clearly was still my daughter. Everything else was still cloudy, the way Heaven was always portrayed in old movies.

"You have a million questions," she said. "There's a million answers waiting for you. But you're not going to get them standing here. Come on."

She took me by the hand and we started walking. I let her guide me.

"Why are you a little girl again?" I asked.

"Because that's the way you've always seen me," Felony said. "Everything you see when you first get here is subjective, dreamlike."

"I'm not seeing what you really look like?"

"Well, you're not seeing me the way everyone else does yet."

"If you're still alive back on earth, how did you get here before I did?"

"Do you really want a lecture on resolving the paradox equations in temporal mechanics five minutes after you get to Heaven? Or is it enough if I tell you that I gave you grandchildren and great-grandchildren before I died?"

I laughed. "Did you make any movies?"

She smiled. "I dedicated my first directing Oscar to you."

"I'm sorry I missed it, sweetheart."

"Who said you're going to miss it?"

"I'll take that lecture now," I said, grinning.

Felony looked at me seriously. "Do you have any idea why you were brought here?"

"You mean *you* don't know?"

She shook her head. "All I know is that I got a message telling me that you were arriving today and asking me to guide you until you're reborn."

I frowned. "You mean I have to go through puberty again?"

She laughed. "No, Daddy. Unless you want to stay a ghost, just using your second body, you need to get new flesh. Which, considering your love for all-you-can-eat restaurants, I don't think you'd like very much. Come on."

"Is it going to hurt?"

"Just because you're being reborn is no excuse to act like a baby," my teenage daughter the grandmother said.

Chapter Four

Have you ever noticed how many different cultures burn candles as memorials or in prayers for the dead? Being an atheist, I'd always looked for rational explanations about stuff like that. Let's say that you're in a society before the invention of cameras, with few people who can even write or paint. What can just about anyone do in remembrance of the dearly departed? About all you could do was to light a candle, that was my way of thinking about it.

If you get nothing else out of this narrative, get this: just about everything is more complicated than I'd thought.

As Felony was leading me by the hand to the appointed place of my rebirth, my inability to see things around me subsided, and I gradually became aware of my surroundings. We were walking along a path in a well-manicured city park, with high-rise architecture surrounding me at a distance.

It was hard for me to assign a style to the buildings. You know how, in the Albert Brooks movie *Defending Your Life,* Judgment City looks like the outskirts of Las Vegas? This was nothing like that. There was little in common with earth styles of architecture at all.

It wasn't the glass-and-steel towers of America, not the classical styles of a European capital, neither the elaborate temples of Asia nor the Moorish edifices of the ancient Near East. It was more self-consciously artistic, with the architect being liberated from the load-bearing requirements of earth construction to explore pure esthetics, and with an astonishing variety of building materials.

Some buildings looked as if they had been grown as a single crystal, the ultimate in organic integrity. There were some structures that looked as if they were constructed of clouds, and a few that had the *Blade Runner* look of a Syd Mead illustration. Some of the more-metallic-looking buildings hovered high above the others, like a cover from a 1940's *Astounding*. The overall effect was like the 1964 New York World's Fair or Disneyland, but done for real.

The building that Felony brought me to near the outskirts of the park looked as if Dr. Seuss or M.C. Escher had a hand in its design. From the outside it looked like a series of glowing mazes that turned in on themselves. But when you passed inside (not through a door; right through what appeared to be a solid wall) it looked a cross between an ancient Roman home and the medical practice of Dr. Victor Frankenstein. I had a real sense that whoever had done the interior decorating had seen way too many movies.

To my right I saw a modernistic waiting room with plush chairs, couches, and coffee tables piled with old magazines that would have looked at home in a dentist's waiting room. The room was full but I didn't have to put my name on a list. Sophia and Estella, the angels who crossed me over, were waiting for me as we entered, both dressed in a translucent white dress that reminded me of a nurse's uniform by way of Hugh Hefner. Either Sophia or Estella would qualify as your average Playmate of the Year. "He's waiting for you," Sophia said.

"Who's waiting?" I asked, but directed the question to my daughter, and suddenly she was no longer 12-years-old but a woman who looked my own age.

"Jesus, of course," Felony said. She kissed me on the cheek. "Call me when you're settled in, Daddy. I'm in the Tree."

Felony disappeared, the way the two angels had when I'd died. It was a bit disconcerting.

"This way, sir," Sophia said. The angels linked arms with me from both sides. I didn't know whether to feel escorted or under arrest.

There's no way to say this that isn't going to tick somebody off, so I'm just going to say it. The Savior looked like a Middle Eastern terrorist or a Colombian drug lord. Or at least that's what he looked like to a Hollywood-imprinted American arriving from the early-21st century.

Jesus looked short, muscular, olive-skinned, with piercing eyes, jet-black hair, and a thick black beard; when I was brought in to him he was wearing a white Sydney Greenstreet suit. The only thing that broke the stereotypical first impression was Jesus' brilliant smile and the bear hug with which he greeted me.

The angels left, closing a door behind them, and Jesus motioned me over to a couple of upholstered chairs, catercorner to each other.

"Mind if I smoke?" Jesus asked.

If I still had one I raised an eyebrow but said, "No problem."

No, I can't tell you what brand of cigarette Jesus

smokes; he took an elaborately carved pipe and a cloth
pouch out of his jacket pocket, packed something pink
and fleshy from the pouch into the pipe, and blew into
the mouthpiece as if it was a child's bubble pipe. It
wasn't bubbles that came out of the pipe's bowl,
though, but a jet of flame followed by a thick cloud of
white smoke.

It didn't smell like tobacco to me, and not like mari-
juana, either, if that's where you thought I was going.
It smelled a little like incense or burning spices but
overall, it smelled to me like barbecue smoke.

I don't know what I'd expected when I sat down in
the arm chair opposite Jesus—maybe a chance to get
a few of my questions answered—but what happened
next was nothing I could have anticipated.

Jesus took a deep draught of smoke from his pipe
and blew it towards me, not a short breath but a deep,
continuing wind that traveled along with a deep low
humming. The smoke began swirling around me,
faster and faster and faster, and a jet of flame formed
above me.

Suddenly it was as if I was a candle, but instead of
rising, the flame started moving downwards, and I felt
intense heat starting at my temple and spreading out
from there to my entire body. But instead of consum-
ing me, the flame was making me solid.

I don't know if I passed out, went into a trance, or
whether it was over in only an instant, but the next
thing I knew the flame was gone, the smoke was floating easily up to a cathedral ceiling ... and I had a solid
body of flesh again. But rebirth doesn't come with
clothes. I was sitting in the arm chair, now naked.

Not for long. Sophia and Estella were right behind me with a terrycloth bathrobe. When I stood up I felt a bit wobbly but managed not to fall. Estella helped me on with the robe ... and just in time, otherwise the Savior would have been staring at a growing erection triggered by my proximity to Estella's cleavage as she bent over to cinch the robe's tie for me.

Sophia placed a golden chalice into my hands, and Jesus picked up one like it. Estella picked up a pitcher and poured a clear liquid into both cups.

"To life," Jesus said to me.

Jesus put the cup to his lips and so did I. We drank. It was a wow. I didn't know what it was but knew that if somebody bottled it on earth, Coca Cola would be out of business.

Jesus stood up, and with some effort I made it back onto my feet.

"I apologize," said Jesus, "but I have a full waiting room. I'll see you in the morning at breakfast, all right?"

"Sure," I said, weakly.

Jesus and I shook hands then Sophia and Estella helped me walk out of Jesus' office ... and directly into what looked to be the master bedroom of my town home back in Culver City.

"Get a good night's sleep and we'll be back for you in the morning," said Estella.

"Sweet dreams," said Sophia, and then, much to my regret, they were both gone.

I went into my bathroom and looked at myself. I didn't look any different than the way I had looked before I died.

I walked to my bedroom window, opened it wide, and looked out, but instead of looking at the garage doors of the next row of houses, I had a spectacular view of the heavenly skyline at night. I wasn't in Kansas anymore, Toto.

Heaven doesn't smell like any other city I've ever visited. There are no industrial fumes; instead, the air is permeated with a spicy, deep-forest fragrance. There was a lovely warm breeze carrying this wonderful air into the house so I decided to keep the window open.

I was more tired than I'd thought. I threw the robe on a chair, climbed into bed, and was asleep before I knew it.

Chapter Five

A lot of people think angels don't have a sense of humor. I don't believe it for a minute.

It must be obvious from this narrative that Sophia and Estella had been assigned to watch over me. Just exactly what that responsibility entails is a matter open to interpretation, but allowing me, while asleep, to float out of my open bedroom window buck-naked to do an aerial tour of the Heavenly City, does not in my opinion qualify as attention to duty.

At the time I departed earth, a lot more about dreaming was mysterious than understood. People tossed around terms like wish fulfillment, R.E.M. cycles, alpha and theta brainwaves, collective unconscious, directed dreaming, and bicameral minds. But the simple fact is that the ancients, who saw dreams as omens or prophecy, at least took what happened during dreaming as something as real as waking states of being. With the exception of the few remaining Australian aboriginals, practically nobody on earth had a clue why human beings were made to dream.

Almost immediately upon my arrival in Heaven, I found out what dreams are for. It was not only an inescapably obvious experience, but it was at the heart of a political struggle that made earthbound conflicts over abortion, Jerusalem, or skin color look like a bingo game by comparison.

The capacity to dream, to *really* dream, is what makes the human race "made in God's image."

I'm not talking about merely replaying waking experiences while asleep. That's one of the lowest lev-
els of dreaming that even a sleeping dog experiences.
I'm not talking about the visiting between those living on earth and loved ones who'd crossed beyond, or
even the antics of otherworldly trespassers who got
off on using human dreamers as their personal entertainment consoles.

The sorts of dreams I mean are the ones that seem
more real and important to you than what happens
when you're awake, dreams that are either a horror
you awaken from with pounding heart and covered
in sweat, or a transcendent bliss that breaks your heart
when you awaken to mundane existence. Some people
have taken dreams this intense to be visits to other
realms, including Heaven and Hell, and in rare cases
they were.

But what God designed dreams to be in his original
specs for the human race is our ability, like God himself, to imagine new worlds into existence.

Not that I learned all this on my first night in Heaven.
What I did learn that night is that the dreams I'd had
as long as I could remember, in which I could fly, came
true once Jesus had given me my new body. My old
body being constructed of matter with the properties
of mass, and consequently gravitationally attracted to
all other masses, was simply not designed to rise out
of a gravity well at will.

Back on earth, some living souls used their dream
states as an opportunity to leave their leaden bodies
behind a short while, for some astral soaring around
the planet, while others flew by ignoring gravity in

dream worlds of their own creation. Speaking for myself, I had a rare night of the first kind, in which I left my body behind in bed and soared above mountains and through cities, and quite a few more of the second, where my ability to fly was an ordinary feature of my created dreamlands.

What I didn't know, when I climbed into bed that first night, is that the new body Jesus gave me wasn't made out of ordinary matter like my old body, and that its mass was a variable designed to be consciously controlled. Once I fell asleep and habitually went into one of my usual flying dreams, my new body automatically responded, and like a sleepwalker, I was propelling myself right out my bedroom window and floating above the treetops.

I was cruising along about a mile high and a couple of hundred miles an hour when Sophia and Estella caught up with me, gently caught me and started guiding me back home, still fast asleep. I awakened at about 3,500 feet up and about fifteen minutes away from my bedroom window to find myself naked but not cold, flying prone with the city lights of Heaven below me, two gorgeous angels as my honor guard, and my pecker pointing down like landing gear.

I didn't have a chance to be embarrassed for very long. As soon as she became aware that I was awake, Sophia laughed merrily then pulled herself close to me, kissing me sensually. Estella joined in kissing me from the other side. I was way distracted after that but I can state with some authority that I wasn't doing any more dreaming that night. I didn't need to.

The science-fiction novelist and folksinger, L. Neil

Smith, once asked in a lyric, "Can you get laid, up in Heaven?"

Believe it or not, even though the opportunity presented itself to me, my first choice wasn't to spend the rest of my first night in Heaven doing a *ménage à trois* with a couple of angelic Playmates. I could *fly*. I hurriedly dressed and I spent the next few hours in flying lessons, soaring above and through the streets of Heaven with the two most beautiful flight instructors I'd ever seen.

While we're on the subject, let's get a few things straight about angels.

Angels don't have wings. They're not burritos like humans; they just use the one astral body, not pulled by gravity. The whole "on wings of angels" thing was a nice poetic metaphor but if you ask me it's gotten a little old.

Angels are neither androgynous nor are they nonsexual beings. It's just that they can choose what sex they want to be. God never neutered them. That tubby bitch Silent Bob got this last part wrong when he made *Dogma*.

Angels are not silent but beautiful sex dolls for humans, either, although I might have given that impression. Sophia and Estella just dug me and it was mutual.

Successful marriages between angels and humans are very rare. If you think the whole *Men are from Mars, Women are from Venus* thing is hard-going communication, try going on a third date when you really *are* from different worlds.

Human writers took the word "angel," which translates as "messenger," then went off on long literary tangents portraying angels as nothing more than God's messengers, choir singers, and clerical staff. Wrong. The race of humanoid spirits we call angels were God's first children, our older brothers and sisters. Sure, they do chores around the house; they're good people and enjoy helping out when they're not too busy with their own stuff. There's a corps of elite angels who serve in the Regiment of the Lord, when God needs soldiers, bailiffs, or police officers. But "angel" isn't a job description. Even in Heaven, the phrase, "You're an angel!" is mostly a term of endearment.

The important difference between humans and angels is that angels are those spirits who have never incarnated into flesh. Angels who have incarnated into flesh are pretty much the same as spirits grown on earth. They wouldn't be angels any more; they'd be human. The angels that have never been human don't sleep; it's not part of their nature. They're alert all the time.

Angels don't dream.

There are angels who are jocks and angels who are nerds. You don't want to go up against an angel in a karate match or on *Jeopardy*; they'll cream you. But psychologically, angels are simply not human.

Angels don't write novels or plays; they write elegant verse, encyclopedias, and history. They are fabulous mathematicians with tons of theorems attributed to them but none of them could have come up with the visualization that led Albert Einstein to $E=mc^2$. They're the best engineers around. Angels make wonderful portrait painters, photographers, and cinematographers; but there isn't a René Magritte or Walt Disney among them. They're terrific dancers but lousy actors; the universe's best Renaissance musicians, circus performers, and Elvis impersonators — this last is the opinion of Elvis, himself — but an angel couldn't write a joke if someone's life depended on it.

That doesn't mean that angels don't laugh or aren't witty; lots of things amuse them—usually human foibles, like my late-night nude excursion. I've been at cocktail parties where I saw angels, in duels of sarcastic banter, one-upping Mark Twain and Oscar Wilde.

I learned the hard way that you don't want to take angels to a comedy club. Once I took Sophia and Estella to a club in the Soho district of Heaven called The Divine Comedy to see the 16th century playwright Christopher Marlowe doing a stand-up routine, and twenty minutes into his act, Marlowe came down to our table and started ragging on me because I kept on having to lean over and explain to the angels why all the humans were laughing. I found out later that the girls had done this sort of thing before and, though they really don't get human jokes, seeing me squirm was how the two of them were getting *their* jollies.

I'm getting ahead of my own story.

Morning came but I wasn't tired. At about 6:30 AM by my living room clock, I took a quick shower, put on my meeting-with-the-affiliates suit, and flew out with Sophia and Estella for my breakfast meeting.

Have you ever noticed that the gospels refer to

Heaven as the Kingdom of God? You wouldn't know it from movies like *Heaven Can Wait*, *Made in Heaven*, or *What Dreams May Come*. You don't see God playing any part in Hollywood's version of Heaven. It's a curious omission.

Heaven is a kingdom. God is the king. The Lord's palace is at the very center of the city and is Heaven's main tourist attraction.

What everything that had happened to me added up to, since line seven had lit up in the K-TALK studio, was that Duj Pepperman had been given a royal summons to appear at court that morning at 0800 hours Celestial Standard Time.

A number of traditions—Gnostic, Hermetic, Masonic — refer to God as the Great Architect of the Universe. Nowhere is this observation truer than in the design of God's own home.

The Heavenly Palace is an enormous diamond whose lowest point hovers about fifteen feet — exactly ten cubits — off the ground. Think of the structure as two Great Pyramids joined together at their base, floating in the air, with the apex of one pointing up and the apex of the other pointing down.

Each facet of the diamond lights up in an ever-changing pattern of colors, so that the overall impression from any approach is that you're looking at a display that combines the drama of never-ending fireworks with the intricacy of a Bach cantata.

On official occasions when God is holding open court, each of the facets becomes a view screen, and you can watch the proceedings from just about anywhere in the city.

Like the entrance to Jesus' resurrection clinic, there are no doorways. You fly up to any outside surface and simply pass through to the inside.

The space inside the palace seems to operate on its own physical laws. You simply can't get anywhere inside where you're not invited; if you tried, you'd simply find yourself outside the diamond again, with the possibility that the outside surface wouldn't open to you any more.

From whatever point public visitors enter the palace from the outside, they end up at the same reception hall inside, reminiscent of the lobby to a great museum.

The palace is a city within a city. Of course there's the Great Hall where God holds court in the grand style, as well as God's own personal residence and the private offices, apartments, and conference facilities used by the palace staff. Several museum-worthy collections housed within the palace are open to the public—art, historical displays, and a pavilion dedicated to the Lives of the Saints, as well as research facilities available to scholars who have been cleared for high-level-access in the Tree of Knowledge. There's a library with every book or film that's ever been burned on earth, including the missing works of Socrates, Plato, Aristotle, and others that were destroyed in Alexandria.

The palace also has 46 public restaurants ranging from fine dining to snack bars, and there are angels who act as docents for tours of the palace's museums and ceremonial facilities, when not in official use. There's even a souvenir kiosk where you can pick up miniatures of the palace, art reproductions, toys, and the inevitable shirts that read, "My parents went to Heaven and all I got was this lousy T-shirt."

Sophia and Estella had security clearance to bypass the reception area and shepherd me directly from outside the diamond into God's living room.

I don't know what I was expecting from God's personal digs, but this wasn't it. There weren't any fancy Louis XVI chairs or long halls with huge oil paintings; no displays of fine bone china or carved ivory miniatures; no desks with inlaid mahogany. The only obvious ostentation was shelf after shelf displaying books, musical albums, and movies. It's a habit of mine to check out what people keep on their home shelves; it's often a glimpse into their personality. God's living room has the best collection of science-fiction and fantasy I've ever seen outside of the Ackermansion, but his listening tends toward music salad, from Camille Saint-Saëns to Stevie Wonder, from Dmitri Shostakovich to Astor Piazzolla, from Vince Guaraldi to Alanis Morissette. Chris Isaak's song "Wicked Game" was playing when I came in. *Uh oh*, I thought.

The place wasn't designed for show but for creature comfort. There were plush couches and even plusher recliners, an extensive wet bar, a long table heavy with bowls of fresh fruit, candy bars, cheeses, crackers, potato chips, dips, and bottled soft drinks on ice.

There was a huge roman bathtub with massage jets, enormous stereo speakers in each corner, and the biggest flat-screen I'd seen anywhere.

You know how there are places in dreams that you

keep on going back to, that you can describe in detail as easily as places you've lived, but that you know you've never been to before? Suddenly I had the strongest flash of déjà vu I'd ever experienced.

I'd lived in this room, in my dreams.

But that momentary precognition made it only slightly less shocking to me when God walked into the room, obviously the Lord of the palace because he was barefoot and wearing a silk kimono. God waved to Sophia and Estella, then grinned widely when he saw what had to be the queerest expression on my face when I first saw him.

Aside from my being overweight, I was an identical twin of God.

Chapter Six

"Hi, I'm God," said God, extending his hand to me.

I didn't faint, though I think I had every right to. I was also completely tongue-tied for the first time I could remember.

I could see Sophia and Estella enjoying my predicament, but they managed to contain themselves.

"Uh, pleased to meet you," I managed to croak, my radio voice gone for the moment. I managed to stay on my feet, took his hand, and shook it.

"Make yourself comfortable," God said. *"Mi casa su casa.* I had my angels bring you here a little early so we could chat a bit privately before my wife and son join us for breakfast."

"You're ... married?" I asked.

God nodded. "I had the Hebrews start their calendar on my wedding day so I'd never forget an anniversary."

God noticed the expression on my face. "What?" he said.

"Uh, aside from the idea that God has a human body and a wife, I'm just a bit thrown off by the idea that you need a calendar to remember anything," I said. "I didn't know you could forget."

God opened a bottle of juice and poured it over two glasses of ice, handing me one. "It's the same nectar Jesus gave you that you liked so much," he said.

"Thank you," I said, taking the glass.

"You're welcome," God said. He motioned me to a

recliner facing an outside view of the city, and sat down in one right next to it, leaning back and putting his feet up. "You're right. I can't really forget anything," he said. "But I can get so focused on a project that I might need a reminder to widen my perspective again. You were married. You remember how that annoyed your wife." God took a sip of his drink and put the glass down on the armrest of his chair. "Ask your burning question," he said.

"Since you're God, who am I?"

"Who, indeed?" said God. "Yesterday, while sitting in a restaurant on earth, you remembered that you are God and experienced godlike powers of cognition. Just now you learned that you look and sound exactly like God, too. You've dreamt of living here. Two of my best angels have been treating you like you're God. Yet, you haven't felt much like God since you drowned—in fact you're quite frightened. The only continuity of identity you have is Duj Pepperman. You're self-conscious about all your ungodly imperfections. You feel powerless. You take notice that I live here in this magnificent palace at the center of Heaven and you don't. Does that about sum up the paradox of your question?"

"Oh, yes," I said. "Can I add the observation that, like me, you also have a fondness for long monologues?"

God grinned. "And, you have my chutzpah," he said, sipping his nectar again. "What I'm about to tell you is unrecorded in any earthly scripture. You can find clues in the Christian gospels, many more in Gnostic texts, but any religious scholar on earth, clerical or lay, would regard a clear statement of the purpose for your very existence as the foulest heresy, the sort of blasphemy they still execute people over, in some quarters. This had to be kept secret from everybody on earth, including you."

I didn't say anything. God was right. I was now too frightened to talk.

"You're my back-up copy, Duj," God said. "Heaven is about to fall into civil war and I cloned you in case I'm captured by the enemy."

I hope nectar doesn't stain. I dropped my glass on the carpet.

The human drama starts with the words, "In the beginning," but the first thing you have to understand about God is that he always was, he is now, and he always will be. When Moses asked God for his name, God identified himself as, "I Am that Will Be"—which is about as close as God could come to describing the unconditional fact of his existence to a brilliant but pre-scientific revolutionary.

From the cradle of philosophy in ancient Athens to modern rationalist thinkers such as Ayn Rand, the axiom that "existence exists" is the starting point for all philosophical examination. Yet, many secular philosophers thought the existence of God impossible because their logic told them that God couldn't come into existence out of nothingness and any consciousness that arose out of existing nature would be subject to natural laws like we are and therefore neither unconditional nor godlike.

What they failed to consider is that existence itself is conscious: self-aware, contemplative, volitional. The words "existence" and "God" are two words identifying the same axiomatic fact. Existence itself is the body and mind of God.

For unfathomable eons, God's experience of himself was whole and contented. He enjoyed thickening and thinning his body into distinct universes, blowing bubbles that exploded into universes bound by time and space, creating galaxies, stars and planets, watching them do their cosmic dances, then either dissipate back into his body or crunch back together for another explosion and a new dance.

Then God had a philosophical thought, a "what if" speculation, a fantasy, if you prefer. It was a thought that was to change everything, including God's own experience of himself.

"What if," God thought, "I could want something I couldn't have?"

It was an intriguing idea. Since everything that existed was part of God's body and obeyed his every command, how could anything fail to yield to his will? It was like the classic child's question, could God make a mountain so big that he couldn't move it?

Many times had God composed universes the way we would think of a musical composer writing a symphony. God found pleasure in the dialectic of tension and release, dissonance resolving into consonance. There was always a small thrill as God felt a universe crunching to maximum tension, then exploding. God wondered what the thrill of release would be like if there could be an even more intense build up of tension, one he couldn't launch at will.

The new thought was exquisite in the variety of possibilities it raised.

God contemplated the new thought for what even he considered a long time. After contemplating a lot of different possibilities, and even creating and destroying a number of different universes as experiments to verify his thinking, God decided that the only thing that could possibly create the sort of dynamic he was looking for, the only thing that could build up a tension great enough for the sort of thrill he was seeking, would be to split off part of himself into a separate consciousness, independent of himself, a separate consciousness that could say to him, "No."

With the possibility of the first "no" would also be created the possibility of the first "yes."

Thus did the Lord trade his omnipotence, his omniscience, and his omnipresence for the possibility of finding love.

All that followed—the creation of other conscious spirits, the creation of life, the creation of angels and of men, and the even more fabulous opportunity that God offered himself, that he could merge his consciousness into one of his own lesser bodies and live for a time among his own creatures—was an adventure for God. He had given himself the gift of love, but with it came the gift of grief.

Never did God regret his decision. Not for an instant, he told me.

Start with Helen of Troy's beauty but add in Goldie

Hawn's smile. Go next with the body of Rita Hayworth. Mix well with Kathleen Turner's voice, Ayn Rand's intellect, and Audrey Hepburn's charm. Season lightly with the sass of Sandra Bullock or Jenna Elfman and this *might* come close to adequately describing my first impression of God's wife, Maryse.

Breakfast was at a round table in the family room. The table floated without any pedestals to bump knees into and the chairs floated automatically to the right height and distance. Around the table were the holy Trinity: God the Father, Jesus the Son, Maryse the Holy Spirit … and me.

Food service seemed to be via teleportation or some technology unfamiliar to me; either that or God was just creating a smorgasbord off the cuff. Being distracted by the company and the conversation, I don't remember everything I was eating, but I do remember portions of a gingerbread frittata, smoked salmon blintzes with Cointreau sauce, and some fresh fruit that looked like a mango but had the texture and taste of *crème brûlé*.

It wasn't my plan to become the center of conversation, but Maryse had other plans. "I don't believe I've ever heard the name 'Duj' before," she said. "How did you end up being called that?"

I smiled wryly. "It's my own fault," I explained. "My first job out of college was on a small AM station in Riverside during evening drive time. I ran the board, spun records, read news, did a little commentary now and then, and took calls. I was fielding an obnoxious caller who disagreed with one of my commentaries, and he said I was nothing but a stupid disk jockey. I shot back—clever me—that I wasn't a stupid disk jockey, I was a stupid *dusk* jockey, and before too long, 'DJ' became 'Duj' and I was stuck with it."

"That's interesting," she said, smiling warmly, "because my name came about almost the same way. Before I was incarnate my name was Yse." She pronounced it to rhyme with Leesa. "I was named Mary when I was on earth. I couldn't decide which name I wanted to use when I crossed back to the celestial realm so I put them together as Maryse."

God saw that I was still holding my tongue and gave me a look.

I leaned back slightly and shrugged. "It's not that I don't want to ask all three of you questions," I said. "It's that I want to ask *every*thing and I don't know where to start."

"Ask anything, Duj," God said. "That's why you're sitting at this table now. Even though this is new to you, you're family."

"Here goes," I said, turning back to Maryse. "Do you just call your husband 'God' all the time or do you have a nickname for him?"

She grinned at me. "It depends on what sort of mood I'm in. If I feel he's really being pig-headed about something, I call him 'Joe,' because I know it annoys him so much."

I cocked my head to the side. "Joe?"

"Diminutive of 'Joseph,'" she said. "That was God's name when he incarnated on earth."

"Okay, now I'm really getting confused," I said. "I thought *you*," I said indicating God, "incarnated on earth as *you*," I said, gesturing toward Jesus.

"Mmm-hmm," Jesus said, taking half a bagel and shmeering cream cheese on it. "You can blame the Nicean Council in the early fourth century for that one," he said. "You ready for the real story?"

I leaned back and listened to *The Gospel According to Jesus*.

Chapter Seven

And Jesus spake unto me:

In the time before Time, there was but One Spirit and He was Whole and Content. This spirit was my Father, whom you now observe incarnated into a fleshly body of His own design.

My father wished a companion so he split off part of himself and created a free Spirit, the first spirit created free from prior existence becoming the Second Person—my Mother.

My father and mother, God and Goddess, played with Each Other, creating tensions and releasing them pleasurably, and They decided to make their playing with each other even more pleasurable by taking part from each of them and making a Third.

I was the First Child of God and his Goddess—the Third Person in existence, and the First Born of the race of angels that followed.

"Hold up a second," I interrupted. "Christians always refer to you as the Second Person of the Trinity," I said to Jesus. "You're saying you're the Third Person?"

Instead, Maryse answered, "Jesus is the Second Person, if you're considering it as a royal chain of command. I do my best to be apolitical, to reign but not rule. My interests lie in the advocacy of justice."

Jesus continued:

No one then had bodies. We were all free spirits, and gender was not yet invented. Any of us could join for a time with any other, then part again as we willed. You might think this sort of existence was perfect, but it wasn't. We had intellect and we had fun, but we didn't have goals and without goals we did not experience our lives as meaningful.

Mortal or immortal, no one can be content for very long without anything important at stake, and very long comes quickly when you're immortal. We were discontent.

My father and mother saw trouble brewing with their children not having anything meaningful to do, so they decided to do something about it. My father's introspection told him that just as he had arrived at the impulse for creation by contemplating the greater pleasures offered by the tension of denied gratification, in the same way providing the discontented angels with the possibility of denied gratification could provide their existence with a goal, a direction, a purpose. Out of this sense of purpose could grow meaning.

First he decided that the resistance necessary for delayed gratification would require creating a universe with congealed energy and a linear time line, a universe of matter and energy, space and time. He had made galaxies, stars, and planets in his previous experiments, and imported a number of already made ones into this new universe.

He spent a week evolving life on a planet around a

nice, medium-sized star, designed a salad of colorful plants and a menagerie of interesting pets in a self-sustaining, self-replenishing, and homeostatic ecosystem.

Finally, he invented outer bodies that could slow down the frequency of angelic spirits, enabling matter to impose limitations on spirit—making them subject to external forces. He even fashioned a body for himself, and liked it so much that he started wearing it frequently.

On the sixth day, my father opened up Eden, the first ever theme park, and told his children that if they wanted to play in it we'd have to put on these cute new bipedal mammalian bodies he'd evolved for us to use while in the park. What they didn't tell us kids was that it wasn't just a playground. Eden was a kindergarden that taught through educational games, with the purpose of teaching little angels how to grow up to be big gods.

"But something went wrong," I said.

"Not some*thing* went wrong," said Jesus. "*I* went wrong. I was the first born. I claimed my rightful place as the first angel to put on a body. You know me by still another name, the name on the body I put on. Adam."

His appearance morphed. Now he was taller, clean-shaven, fairer, more Nordic-looking.

"You ate the fruit from the tree with the knowledge of good and evil?"

"That's a nice way of putting it," said Adam.

Visits to Eden were set up on the buddy system. We angels each had to pair up with another buddy and put on matching bodies—one male, one female. My buddy was my best friend, Lucifer, an angel who was just a little younger than me. You guessed it. Lucifer became Eve.

Lucy was always the life of any party, the sort of angel it was always fun to be around. But she always knew I was a sucker for a game of Truth or Dare. She dared me to hack into the project Eden folder of the Tree of Knowledge—Dad's Macintosh computer, if it helps you to think of it that way—where we found an as-yet unimplemented design for dihydrogen monoxide crystals. Snow. Lucy immediately thought of all the fun possibilities. Skiing. Sledding. Snowball fights. Making snowmen and snow angels.

You were a teenager once, you know what it's like. Once Lucy and I got the idea stuck in our heads it seemed like wicked fun. We goaded each other into it and neither of us wanted to back down and look chicken. Our reptile brains — the serpent of legend — were tempting us.

Lucy didn't know her way around the Tree and I did. To continue the metaphor, she was computer illiterate and didn't know how to get past Dad's passwords and safeguards. When it came time to go beyond joking around with each other and actually hack into the planetary operating system, I was the one who knew how to do it and did it.

So, I captured a moon, did a little work on the earth's

orbit, and the next time Dad put on his body and came down to Eden for a walk through the park, I started up the snow machine and told him to look at how Lucy and I had 'improved' on his design.

"Did you spank them?" I asked God.

God didn't answer but shot me a look suggesting my question was boorish. Yes, God had said "ask anything," but maybe I had gone just a bit too close to the line. Maryse, who has perfect manners, pretended not to notice my *faux pas*.

"No, Duj," Jesus said, saving me. "Actually, Dad and Mom were pretty understanding about the whole thing, considering how totally I'd screwed things up. I'd introduced what amounted to a destructive virus into earth's ecosystem, resulting in an ecology spiraling wildly out of control and, just a few hundred years later, in a global deluge."

"Jesus!" I said involuntarily.

He nodded and continued:

But worse than that, I'd screwed up the Great Plan.

Lucy and I stayed on earth in our new fleshly bodies in the company of other angels who had incarnated in the park, but Dad told us if we stayed, it was under the condition that we had our access level in the Tree of Knowledge reduced until we returned to the Celestial Realm. I'd crashed Eden's self-sustaining ecosystem and we were going to have to build a new colony on earth ourselves, by hand. We had to

learn whatever lessons the earth had to give us without being able to check our answers by looking in the
back of the book. No more angels would be allowed
to join the colony until we had things working again;
we were going to have to rely on the labor of our own
human children.

Things got pretty bad. There was a lot of disagree-
ment among those of us now on our own about what
to do. There was a lot of infighting, splitting off into
warring factions. You probably already know that
things turned violent right from the start, when one
of Lucy's and my sons killed his brother over something as silly as which one had cooked my dad a better dinner during a visit.

Lucy was never quite the same after Cain killed his
brother. She withdrew into herself and barely talked
to me. She wanted to take off her body and return to
the Celestial Realm. She had grown to hate earth and
thought the whole Eden project was a mistake from
the beginning. I insisted that there was still work to
be done on earth. We had those stupid sorts of arguments husbands and wives get into where each of us
was accusing the other of having caused the whole
mess. Finally Lucy decided to abandon her body and
returned to the Celestial Realm without me.

I stayed on earth with our kids until my own body
aged beyond repair, then I returned to the Celestial
Realm, leaving my human children even more on their
own. With little more than a few simple rules to keep
them on track, the human race fell into every sort of
corruption possible.

Having lived forever, my father has a lot of patience,

and isn't one to give up or give in. If you read the Old Testament you get a pretty good idea how badly it went, how all the choices Dad had left were between bad and worse. My father was determined to get the Eden project back on track, no matter what it took, even if he had to start all over again. The worst of the lot had to be culled—forced out of their bodies and wait-listed for reincarnation — and Dad made lemonade out of the lemon I'd given him by allowing the deluge I'd caused to clean the planet of all but the best samples. There were several more times when cities of totally corrupt humans had to be culled—Sodom and Gomorrah, Canaan — but it was a holding action, at best.

It took my father a while to figure out a plan then he and mom talked it over for a while and brought it to me to see if I was willing to make up for my mistake. It was going to take all three of us, working as a team, if this was going to work. It was the last chance to save not only earth and my children now living there but the future for all the angels as well. I was so ashamed about my celestial stupidity back in the original park that I agreed eagerly, without even asking what exactly I was going to have to do.

I found myself regretting that rash decision more than once, after I found out what I'd agreed to.

Jesus continued:

"When the time came to execute the new plan, my father visited his spirit into a man named Joseph and my mother visited her spirit into a woman named

Mary. Both of these humans had been approached by angels in advance to make sure they didn't mind the joinings. You know exactly what it feels like because it happened to you for a few minutes yesterday, right?"

I nodded. "Except I wasn't asked in advance whether I minded or not."

"Well," Jesus asked, "did you mind?"

I laughed. "You might as well ask whether I like flying, sex, or ice cream. I think I'd give anything to experience that 'joining' again."

"I knew that," God said to me.

Maryse gave her husband a look and punched him playfully on the arm.

Jesus continued, "While incarnate, they conceived a man child on earth, into whom I breathed my soul at the moment of birth. This was something entirely different than just putting on a body, the way I'd done the first time. I was the first spirit who, having been created in the celestial realm, was naturally conceived and born a mortal human being. I was made to be the first angel ever to die, the first angel ever to go on a suicide mission."

"How did you stand it?" I asked.

"By the skin of my teeth," Jesus said. "Just barely. Scared out of my wits when the time came close."

"Then why did you go through with it?" I asked.

Because it was my fault in the first place! Because it had to be done and there just wasn't anyone else qualified for the job. Keep in mind, nothing like this had ever been tried before. If something went wrong, existence itself might have been damaged beyond repair. But if it worked—if it could *work*—then all of us, angels and humans, could take on the power of imagination—learn how to dream—and be able to create universes of our own.

After the small original colony of angels had cast off their flesh and returned to the Celestial Realm, the human children that we angels had procreated on earth lived in a fleshly body that died, was a ghost for a while—sometimes wandering the earth, sometimes hanging around in dismal cities of the dead—and were wait-listed for a chance to reincarnate on earth and do it all over again. No future to speak of.

I came back to earth to bring the children of earth the good news that my father was granting them conditional amnesty and would take them into his kingdom if they'd simply agreed to get with the program again. I had to be born human rather than merely take over a ready-made human body because I was the test pilot to show the human children that they could be transported to the Celestial Realm where they could be given new bodies, grow spiritually, and evolve into gods.

They saw me die. I was dead. There wasn't any question about it. Then they saw me alive again in a couple of days, looking like myself, without having to be reincarnated as a baby. No less a convincing demonstration of the possibility of resurrection would have worked.

But that was only part of my father's plan.

Evolution into godhood was once again being offered to the angels. Angels could have their spirits incarnate on earth into human bodies, just like in the original Eden project. Angels who haven't yet become human first don't dream. As spirits they lack imagination. Without imagination, creation is impossible.

We were offering angels a chance to become human for a time, so they could learn to dream, and when they returned to the Celestial Realm, they also could become gods.

My father's great plan was the goal of the modern revolutions: liberty, equality, fraternity. The creator of the universe, the author of history, the inventor of life, the father of the races of angels and humans, was also the first revolutionary. If my father's plan worked, the Original Spirit would not only have a companion, children, students, and servants. For the first time, God could have *friends*.

"But no matter what it is, there's always some malcontent, the fly in the ointment, a critic," said Jesus.

"Lucifer?" I guessed.

Jesus nodded. "Lucy. Eve. My best friend. The love of my life. The mother of my children. The worst pain in the ass on earth or in Heaven."

"Your ex-wife," I said, understanding completely.

Chapter Eight

The Trinity told me at the end of breakfast that it was time I got a good look around Heaven on my own, see what was brewing, form my own opinion. None of the three of them expected me to take what Jesus had told me on faith. After intervening directly into human affairs for a few thousand years and seeing how little could be achieved that way, God now takes independence of thought to the extreme and expects people to come to their own conclusions.

But after what I saw, I started wondering, myself, whether it was God who was making a mistake by taking us on faith, expecting the rest of us to be as decent, smart, and reasonable as he was.

I was concerned that looking like God would make me conspicuous as I tooled around Heaven. God assured me that I didn't have to worry, not in a city where God impersonators nightly performed in revues and comedy clubs, where God bodies were the most popular Halloween costume every year, and where every Friday night the midnight show at the Rialto attracted hundreds of fans in full God regalia to lip-synch to the cult movie, *God: The Musical.* "Every once in a while," God told me, "I still go to the midnight show, pick a seat somewhere in the middle, and sing along." He grinned. "I haven't been recognized yet."

Maybe God wasn't recognized but I wasn't out on the streets of Heaven more than a week when I was.

I was having a cappuccino a few blocks from the

palace, sitting at a booth in a HoJo's Jr., thumbing through a copy of Satan's number-one-best-selling autobiography titled *Lucifer is My Slave Name*, when I heard a voice from my past. "Duj? Duj Pepperman? Is that you?"

I turned around to see the smiling face of Iceman Shnull, my co-host on a morning drive show we'd done together in San Antonio for six years, who had been killed at 28 by a drunk driver, twenty years before I passed. He still looked as young as ever.

"Well in the name of God, if it isn't the Iceman!" I said, standing up.

"I thought it was you!" Iceman said, hugging me. "You look like crap, pal, but I'd know your face anywhere!"

So much for anonymity.

Iceman slipped into the booth opposite me and dropped a piece of plastic with the order number 42 onto the table.

"What are you doing nowadays?" I asked him, sitting down again.

"I'm on-camera talent for Heavenly News Network," he said. "I do remotes, mostly entertainment premieres, but lately with what's been going on, I've been doing more hard news breaks. What about you? Still doing talk?"

"Well, I was," I told him. "Then I got carjacked in the parking lot of Jerry's Famous Deli and suddenly I'm out of a job."

Iceman grinned.

An angel brought over a tray with his order, fried clams, a side of welsh rarebit, and a thick chocolate malt. "You eating?" he asked me.

I shook my head. "That's all I've been doing since I got here," I said. "Been eating so much, now that I won't get any fatter, that I think I'm ready to hurl."

"Yeah, everybody does that at first," he told me. "But in a couple of more weeks you'll settle down and get the hang of it. Hey, isn't being able to fly even better though?"

"If I'd known how much fun it is," I joked, "I would've killed myself years ago." I'd already found out by reading in the Tree that you couldn't get past final judgment into Heaven if you'd killed yourself ... at least not without a good lawyer.

"Listen, I'm on a quick break before I have to head back to work," Iceman said. "I'm covering Satan's big Anorexic Party rally at Judas Park this afternoon. I can lend you an HNN press badge and slip you into the press section. You want to come?"

Of course I took the Iceman up on his invitation. This was exactly the sort of thing God told me I was supposed to be checking out.

Iceman and his crew set up their telepresence pickups with dozens of other networks right in front of the band box while I found myself an empty chair a few dozen feet farther back, sitting with the radio commentators and print reporters.

I felt conspicuous about my appearance when a beefy angel, one of Satan's roadies, gave me a weird look. I gestured at the spare tire around my middle and shrugged; the roadie laughed, gave me a thumbs up, and went back to putting up seating on the platform behind Satan for her personal guests.

"Why does God permit suffering?" Satan asked, her hands raised to the skies of Heaven dramatically. "Permit suffering? *Permit* suffering? God was *counting* on suffering! God thinks suffering is *good* for you! Perfection wasn't good enough for God. God didn't *like* perfection. The entire fucking idea behind creation was to fuck things up as much as possible and make everyone else's life a living *hell*!"

The multitude at the huge rally, tens of thousands of angels but with a surprising number of saved humans mixed in, roared in unison, "Say-*tun*! Say-*tun*! Say-*tun*!"

There's no kind way of saying this so I'll just say it. Satan looked like hell. She was painfully gaunt and sickly looking, her reddish-blonde hair hung down limply, her pale skin hung on her loosely, and she tried to cover up the physical decay by wearing a long black dress and a black beret tilted to the side.

"And at the end of the day, what are these great gifts that God has given us? To make us into animals that were designed only to eat other living things and turn them into shit?"

"No!" the crowd shouted.

"To go through life on earth, ignorant of the truth and scared that we were made from dust only to be turned back into dust ... only to find out that we don't really die forever and it was all just God's little practical joke?"

"No!"

"To have sex—with physical organs, may I remind

you, that God thought so little of that he made them do double duty with pissing and shitting—so we can fall in love with someone who, if you don't get sick to death of each other while smelling each other's farts and bad breath, is going to die and leave you feeling that everything that makes life joyful has come to an end?"

"No!"

"And why? For what? Why did God put all of us through this?" Satan asked the crowd.

"So God could jack off!" an angel in the front shouted.

The crowd roared its approval.

Satan laughed. "You know already. You're with me before I open my mouth. I don't even have to tell you any of this. That's right. God is a thrill junkie, a sex addict, a maniac who runs experiments that destroys other people's lives without even having the decency to warn them of the risks. The Larry Flynt who lives in that floating pleasure palace with that sluttish sex goddess he calls your mother ... and their misbegotten bastard — that middle Eastern terrorist from Central Casting — who claims to be your savior ... are Dr. Frankenstein, the Bride of Frankenstein, and their monster!"

Satan raised her hands again.

The crowd chanted in unison, "Say-*tun*! Say-*tun*! Say-*tun*!"

Satan lowered her arms and waited for silence.

"All of this is so we can follow in Daddy's footsteps and became dreamers. We're supposed to think that if we just put our noses to the grindstone and study the Tree of Knowledge that we'll all be able to make pretty little universes of our own. Well, I've been there and done that. I followed the program. I became a human being. I learned how to dream. I created a universe of my own. And I'm here to tell you that it's not only an *impossible* dream, creating a universe of your own is a nightmare for everybody involved! Why do you think I named the universe that I created, using God's own blueprints, *hell*?"

The crowd roared with laugher.

Satan lowered her voice, almost to a whisper.

"Is this right? Is this fair? After seeing how this great experiment called creation has worked, are you still going to mindlessly stand there like stunned sheep and say to me, 'In God we trust?'"

The crowd laughed uproariously.

"Or are you going to use the one gift that Heaven's own version of Bill Gates gave you that actually has some value? The power to say no? Do you want this nightmare to continue forever or do you want to claim your right to be master of your own destiny? Do you want to stick with this prepackaged, preplanned, one-size-fits-all monopolistic beta test that I like to call *Universe 2000* — "

"Say-*tun*! Say-*tun*! Say-*tun*!"

"—Or do we say that we've simply had enough of being ruled by a tyrant, demand free and honest elections, and run things ourselves?"

"Say-*tun*! Say-*tun*! Say-*tun*!"

Satan pursed her lower lip, stuck out her chin, and extended her right arm out to the mass crowd standing before her in a grand salute.

Chapter Nine

To be perfectly honest, I was pretty shaken up by the Anorexic Party rally. Lucifer was a powerful speaker and a charismatic presence.

A phrase I had learned from reading Ayn Rand, back in my college days, came back to me, "The hatred of the good for being the good."

Lucifer hadn't lied about God's "sexual" motive for creation. The same dialectic of tension-and-release that makes sex pleasurable also makes music pleasurable.

Simply, Lucifer had been putting everything God had done in the worst possible light, rendering no respect or gratitude to God for the simple fact that if it was not for his creative impulses, his willingness to take risks, to be inventive, to take action rather than do nothing, Lucifer would not have even existed to raise her foul-mouthed objections.

After the crowd broke up, I said a quick thanks to the Iceman for getting me into the rally and flew back to my town home to finish reading Satan's own *"Mein Kampf."*

Lucifer was a persuasive writer, but the very clarity of her vision is what made me understand how evil it was down to its very roots.

I understood, perhaps for the first time, that while procreation is driven by the female seduction of the male and the female nurturing of the young, the male willingness to explore, to invent, to face the unknown

down, to be "men of action'—all of which require brav-
ery, boldness, and utter risk-taking—were what drove
males from God on forward to create the new.

Now I knew why western religions all insisted,
counter-intuitively to the observation of nature, that
God was male. Real creation is a violent invasion of
the way things already are, and females are by nature
neither violent nor invaders.

Of course this doesn't mean that females can't be
creative and males can't be nurturing. We each contain, to a lesser extent, the attributes of the other gender. But purely for identifying the principles involved,
creation is the male principle and procreation is the
female.

Lucifer, by any of the names she had used at one
time or another—Eve, Lilith, Satan—hated God because by nature he was more spontaneously creative,
more comfortable in the role of creator, than she was.
Creation seemed easy for God. Lucifer had to work at
it.

Lucifer was jealous of God because when it came
to composing universes, God was Mozart and she was
Salieri.

Lucifer's own effort at creating a new universe of
her own — which she named "Hell" as a compliment
to the ancient Greek philosophers — was a good example. I've had it independently corroborated that the
account she gave in her book, telling what went wrong
with Hell, was pretty honest.

After her life on earth as Eve, Lucifer concluded
that what she had witnessed going wrong on earth
had been the human tendency to focus on the differ-

ences between people rather than their similarities. People fell into an "us versus them" mentality. There were your own tribesmen; everyone else was a barbarian, a *ferengi*, a *gaijin*, a gentile — an outsider. Men focused on the differences they had from women, and vice versa, rather than each focusing on their common humanity and symbiotic roles. Men, in particular, focused on their differences and fought wars over them against other men.

When she decided to create a universe of her own, Lucifer's conception was elegant and, in my opinion, very bold. She decided to make all of her creatures hermaphroditic—capable of either fertilizing others or being fertilized to bear children themselves—and to make all of them physical twins to each other. It would be an entire planet of twin siblings whom, she believed, would have no differences to fight about.

Brilliant in conception as it was, Hell was a disaster.

The principle of uniformity started out bad and, as it evolved, only got worse. Without individual distinctions, everybody saw everybody else as a spare part, to be thrown away as soon as the slightest defect showed up. The social order quickly drifted into an insect-like totalitarianism that made the liquidations of Mao, Stalin, Hitler, and Pol Pot, in our own history, look like the work of amateurs. With no individuality built into the system, there wasn't a single revolutionary capable of the independence of mind necessary to lead a liberation movement to save that world from its own dead end.

They say the road to Hell is paved with good intentions. Lucifer, the Goddess of Hell, found out the truth of that bit of wisdom the hard way—and she felt so guilty over the misery that resulted from her own creation that she decided to start questioning the principle of creation, itself.

It was a short slippery slope from creative frustration to jealousy to a rejection of all she saw around her. It was not by accident that she named her anti-God political movement the Anorexic Party. It was not just that those who rejected God were spitting out the food of life. It was that they were spitting at the king of all invention.

I was so shaken up that I needed to get my mind off politics, even if for a few hours. I got my daughter's number from the Tree, gave her a call, and made plans with her to attend the violin competition of the Heavenly Olympics that evening. Heaven follows the original Greek Olympics in that events are not only athletic but also artistic.

We noticed a lot of celebrities in attendance, but I have to admit I was a bit surprised to see John F. Kennedy sitting in a box with Jackie. I hadn't known the two of them were an item again.

The Olympic Violin competition that night was wonderful, with contestants playing everything from Bach to Bluegrass. As usual, the judges were themselves past violin competition gold-medalists such as Niccolò Paganini, Joseph Joachim, Jascha Heifetz, Isaac Stern and Fritz Kreisler. The gold that night went to a rookie, barely up from earth, named Julie Schulman, who brought the stadium to their feet with his bravura performance of Hoagie Carmichael's third violin concerto.

After the concert, Felony and I went flying into the Sinai mountains for a midnight picnic, and I finally got a chance to catch up with what my daughter had been up to recently. She had written a comic screenplay titled *Alas Poor Eunuch* that William Shakespeare had committed to direct because she was preoccupied writing another script, and the two of them were in a dispute about casting.

"These Brits are such snobs," Felony complained. "Bill wants an actor he worked with at the Globe for the lead, but I had Groucho in mind when I *wrote* the script and I don't give a damn that Groucho's not 'classically trained.' If Shakespeare doesn't back down, I'm going to ask my co-producer, George Lucas, to fire him while we're still in pre-production and see if we can get Nora Ephron."

When I got home that night at about 0300 CeST, there was a message on my phone from God's appointment secretary, Ruth, asking me to come back to the palace for a meeting with God at 0900 that morning. I decided I had time for a few hours shut-eye so I set my alarm for 0700 and sacked out.

It seemed to me that I'd only been asleep for a few minutes, though, when I felt a huge *crack* and my bed started shaking. The first thought in my head was *earthquake* and my California instincts took over immediately. I flew, literally, under the nearest doorway and waited for the rumbling to die down.

But when I looked out my window, what I saw filled me with horror.

The gigantic diamond palace at the center of

Heaven—the seat of the Throne of God — was missing from the night sky ... and the streets below where it had been were on fire.

Chapter Ten

In the skies above Heaven's burning streets, some of Satan's partisans were skywriting, *God is dead—Nietzsche lives.*

I'd been an atheist for all but the last few minutes of my earthly life and on earth I had never felt I needed guidance from God. But after just one meeting with God and his family, I felt lost without them. It would be a tragic irony beyond belief if I'd learned the truth about the existence of God just before God ceased to exist.

Of course I didn't know that God was dead, or even if God could die. God had told me the very reason for my own existence was as a back up for the contingency that he was captured by the enemy. But if God had been captured, what could I possibly do about it? Even already dead, I was still scared to death. Had God given up so much of his power and vision that he could be blindsided by an attack before he had a chance to meet me that morning? And what was the purpose of that meeting, anyway?

I started to realize that I was panicking when I saw a red glow being projected on the walls of my bedroom, and realized it was coming from *me*. I looked in the mirror and saw that I was flashing like a neon sign.

So I took steps to calm down. I took a step back. I consciously tried to relax. I didn't even know whether I had a heart anymore (I'd been so busy since I got to

Heaven that I didn't even have a chance to read the
user's manual for my new body; it was still sitting
unopened on my bedside table) so I took the deep
breaths that in my old body would have slowed my
pulse. It worked. I stopped glowing and calmed down.

Hey, regardless that my town home was across the
border in Culver City, I was an *Angeleno*. As a radio
personality I'd handled earthquakes, brushfires,
mudslides, riots, and Barbra Streisand's political pro-
nouncements. There wasn't *any* disaster I couldn't
handle.

I needed more information.

Since I wasn't on the air myself, I turned on the TV,
just at the right time to catch breaking news on HNN:
a press conference by Satan.

Satan walked out with what looked to be her general staff lined up behind her. She looked as if she'd
had a sleepless night. For some reason that was not
apparent to me, the emotions she was projecting were
not in agreement with the message she was delivering. She was about to declare victory but she looked
as if she was giving a concession speech.

"I'm not taking any questions yet," she said, then
put on a pair of eyeglasses and read from a prepared
statement.

"The Throne has surrendered Heaven," read Satan,
quietly but emotionally. "The program of the Anorexic
Party for transfer of power to a popular form of government has been agreed to."

There was a huge roar of approval from the crowd.
Satan waited until it died down to continue.

"I felt it was better to make some minor concessions rather than have to engage in a protracted war of attrition against our brethren still loyal to the Royal Family. Here are the negotiated terms under which we now enter into the era of Heavenly freedom.

"First," Satan said, "The palace has been removed from Heaven into its own dimensional matrix and the Trinity are banned from Heaven. Any angels or humans who wish to join them will be permitted to do so while the tunnels are still operating. We have been assured by the Throne that there is enough spacetime within the palace to accommodate comfortably all angels and resurrected humans who wish to join them.

"Second, with respect to the territories of earth, we have agreed to an earthly Interregnum for the Reformation period of the Christian epoch, at the end of which the future control of earth will be determined by a popular election for the governorship of earth. Qualification for governor shall include only native earthborn, which excludes all previously unincarnated angels; additionally, none of the Trinity may run for this office.

"The Interregnum shall begin Luther 001 at 0900 CeST and end with the election to be held on earth on a date to be mutually agreed to by both parties, who must file before Satan 001 at 0500 CeST. At 1200 hours CeST, all tunnels to earth or to the palace shall go dark. One-way tunnels to transport earthborn souls to Heaven before Satan 001 shall be permitted for the duration of the Interregnum. Those of you not with us: this is your last chance to depart our territory. Outbound tunnels will be off after noon today.

"Also after noon CeST today," Satan continued, "all

access to the Tree of Knowledge shall be shut off, both here and on earth. The Trinity shall be permitted to listen to and answer prayers for comfort from the earth-bound during the Interregnum but neither the Trinity nor our party shall be permitted to perform any miracles above π on the Aquinas Scale for the duration.

"At the end of the Interregnum, elections shall be held on earth, and upon our electoral victory two-way tunnel traffic shall be reactivated for all and the Anorexic Party shall be free to take control of earth in addition to the territories already ceded to us today."

Satan paused for a moment then put away her statement and took off her glasses. "I'll have further statements, and perhaps answer some questions, later this afternoon, after I have a chance to consult with my kitchen cabinet. That's all for now."

The crowd erupted into shouts of "Say-*tun*! Say-*tun*! Say-*tun*!"

Lights flashing, Satan walked off the podium, her retinue following.

I couldn't believe it. How could God just run away like that, giving up to someone as evil as Satan without a fight?

It just didn't make sense. But it was about to. Big time.

My doorbell played the chimes of Big Ben. I opened my front door. It was Sophia and Estella. I let them in.

"We have a recorded message for you," Sophia said.

A holographic image of the Trinity appeared in front of me, backlit as if in solar eclipse. I saw my daughter Felony standing off to the side.

It was way too bright. I needed to shield my eyes.

Estella saw my problem, waved a hand in front of my face, and my eyes adjusted properly.

And God spoke:

"My son, I know you're frightened right now. You're just now coming to realize that I've been watching over you for your entire life, even though you didn't know it, and now you will learn that I'm going to have to leave you on your own for a while.

"I know you're going to find this hard to believe but even I can be afraid. Especially I can be afraid. I have more reasons to be afraid than anybody because I have more that I love at risk than anybody else. It's all right to be afraid. Just don't let your fears get the better of you.

"I would have preferred to tell you this in person but events have come to pass sooner than I would have hoped, though not sooner than I prepared for.

"I'm sending you on a mission of vital importance. You must return to earth before the tunnels are shut down at noon today. Sophia and Estella will see you safely back to earth but they may not stay there with you. Be certain of this: everything you need to know, everything you need to know how to do, is already within you. You do not need to look to the Tree for guidance. All of the Tree that you need is within you.

"You are to be our Ambassador Plenipotentiary to earth, with full authority to act in our name and to make binding commitments on our behalf. To put it another way, you are the campaign manager for the Party of God in the upcoming gubernatorial election that will determine the fate of earth. The outcome of that election will in turn determine the fate of the rest of my creation.

"I give you these blessings to help you on your mission:

"First, look for a circle to form around you.

"Second, don't make campaign promises I'm not going to be able to keep.

"Third, feel free to ask for advice, but when it comes time to do your job, you're the only one qualified to do it.

"Fourth, resist not evil.

"And fifth ... use the Force!"

God smiled at me.

"Your daughter will be safe here with us so you don't have to worry about her being used as a hostage.

"I'm betting everything on you, Duj. You are my ultimate go-for-broke: all my cash bet on one horse to win. You have all of our blessings, all of our love, and all of our faith."

The image faded.

"We must fly, sir," Sophia said to me, "if Estella and I are to have time to make it back to the palace from earth before the tunnels are shut down."

I had never been a religious man but I crossed myself.

"But, sir, you've never been a Catholic," Sophia said to me.

I grinned as bravely as I knew how. "You ever try to make a Star of David on your chest?" I asked, knowing she wouldn't get the joke. "Come on. Let's get the hell out of here."

Part 2
Back to Earth

Chapter Eleven

I hate traffic jams.

I hate them especially when they're caused by bureaucratic stupidity, like scheduling most Interstate repaving during the summer months when more people are driving cross-country. I know it's because the tar they use can't be poured in cold weather but can't they get Dupont to whip up a better concrete?

I hate that highway engineers have never been allowed to implement a traffic flow system that doesn't permit the failure of one or two vehicles to cripple the entire system during peak loads.

I especially hate the waiting caused by toll booths, which is the bureaucrat's way of saying that their need for sucking a few extra bucks out of you is so important that they don't care how much it ruins your day.

The endless lines of departing angels and humans flying to the tunnels out of Heaven reminded me of the I-10 Freeway east out of Los Angeles on the Friday before Labor Day weekend. If this was an example of how the new leadership was planning to run earth, it was all the more reason to vote against them. Luckily, almost all of the outbound traffic was taking the bypass to the Palace so once Sophia, Estella, and I flew past that exit, the traffic flow sped up considerably.

"Remember to keep your body mass on zero until you're out of the tunnel," Sophia warned me. "Getting stuck inside a black hole is no fun."

"Unless you're on a first date," Estella corrected her.

Sophia and Estella both took positions in front of me, then it was our turn at the departure gate. Sophia jumped, then Estella, and I took up the rear.

I hate trying to follow somebody in traffic. I always lose them.

I took all of two extra seconds in turning myself massless so I could begin accelerating and an angel behind me passed and yelled, "Why don't you learn how to fly?"

"Ah, go *bless* yourself!" I yelled back at him, and hit it, trying to catch up to my guides ... but they were already gone.

Damn! I was about to pull over to the side to figure out what to do when another angel slowed down and paced me. "Lost?"

I nodded, embarrassed. "I was convoying but got left behind. Worse than that, nobody told me my exit."

"Happens to the best of them," he said. "Glide up into the autocontrol lane. The tunnel will read your flight plan and eject you at your destination automatically."

"Thanks!" I said.

"No problem." he said, and sped ahead.

It just goes to show. Don't make any generalizations about angels.

I followed instructions and the autocontrol lane started accelerating me.

It was a quick return trip. The tunnel turned translucent, letting me know that I was about to exit, and I found myself in a glide path coming down over Los Angeles. I felt myself slowing down over Marina del Rey, and hovered for a moment over the roof of Jerry's

Famous Deli, before the tunnel took me through the roof, deposited me inside, floating above the tables, and shrunk to infinity, disappearing.

My mass was still set to zero so for all intents and purposes I was a ghost, invisible to the mortals below me. And, sitting at a table near the bar in Jerry's Famous Deli, was one of those mortals, myself a few days earlier, biting into a tongue and Swiss cheese on rye.

Sophia and Estella had already taken seats at the table where I had originally seen them, when I was the guy at the table eating the sandwich.

At this moment in spacetime there were two of me. The guy sitting at the table, eating the sandwich, was in a mortal body and clueless of what was about to happen to him.

Then there was me, in a resurrected body, with powers and abilities far beyond those of mortal men.

I contemplated the grandfather paradox. What would happen if I killed the living Duj Pepperman right now? Would I still exist? Then I realized it wouldn't make any difference. He was about to die in a few minutes anyway, the "victim" of a carjacking. If I killed him, the worst that would happen would be that he would enter the tunnel a few minutes early and nothing else would have changed.

Lucky for me, I didn't have to test the paradox directly. Estella waved me over and I floated over to their table.

"You need to merge into him so he can see and hear us," Estella told me. "Stay inside him until we hit the water then you'll be free to take his place."

"What about his drowned corpse?" I asked. "The police might find it and it could turn out to be embarrassing for me."

"You never studied," Sophia said disapprovingly.

"Look, I was busy—" I started to explain.

Estella pointed to a dessert list on the table. "What's this?" she asked me.

"A dessert list?" I asked.

"Which is also called a…?"

"Menu?" I responded.

Suddenly, a grid of three-dimensional icons appeared in front of my face along with a virtual mouse. The layout had been copied from my personal computer at home.

"Why don't you run the tutorial before bed tonight?" Sophia suggested.

I nodded sheepishly.

I floated back to the table where the other Duj was eating and merged myself into him.

At the moment that our spirit bodies came into alignment, Duj Pepperman remembered that he was God.

Sophia turned on the radio and tuned it to KLSX FM. The Beach Boys were singing "Good Vibrations."

Both angels started singing along, "I'm pickin' up good vibrations, she's giving me excitations …"

Still singing, Sophia drove onto Admiralty Way. I started singing along with the angels, "Good, good, *good*, good vibrations!"

Sophia turned left on Via Marina, then onto a pier leading out to the harbor. Sophia accelerated the car while opening all four windows. The car leapt the pier and splashed. The Mercedes floated a few seconds then began sinking. Water began rushing in through the open windows.

"Na na na na na ... na na na!" sang Sophia, Estella, the Beach Boys, and me.

It was time for me to leave. I pulled myself out of my old body and floated up toward Sophia and Estella as the Mercedes with my old self in it began sinking quickly.

"I don't like watching this part," I told them. "I felt so scared, so alone."

"Start counting," Estella told me.

"One, two, three ..."

Eight seconds elapsed between my separation from my old body and the moment that Duj cried out "God, where did you go? Why did you leave me?"

Only another six seconds passed before my last words and my last breath.

I'd made the terror last longer than it needed to by holding my breath. At the instant that the rush of cold water hit my lungs, Sophia pulled the old me out of my body and guided him upward while Estella opened a tunnel. All three of us stayed behind his peripheral vision so he wasn't aware of any of us.

I heard him worrying about what would happen to Felony if he died now so I floated over behind him and touched his forehead for a moment to calm him. It worked and he allowed himself to float up to the tunnel and directly into the autocontrol lane.

"Fifty-eight, fifty-nine," I counted.

My old self was gone in sixty seconds.

Estella held the tunnel open for a fast getaway.

"Now if you had *studied*," Sophia told me, "you would have been able to do this yourself already."

She extended her hand and an air bubble formed around the Mercedes, lifting it out of the water; but more than anything else, it looked like a video being run backwards. The Mercedes leapt back out of the water until it was sitting, dry and undamaged, on the pier. There was nobody in it and no body in it. The engine was still running.

"See you soon," Estella said to me. Each of them gave me the sort of kiss that made sure I could never forget them.

"Soon for you or soon for me?" I asked her.

"Is there any difference?" she answered, then Sophia and Estella flew up into the tunnel and it once again disappeared.

I was floating above the Marina, alone.

"Menu," I said, and the display appeared in front of me. I clicked on "My Body" and a mass scale came up. I slowly turned up the mass on my body until I floated slowly down to the pier, and stood there until the scale read "100% Earth normal."

I climbed into the driver's seat of my Mercedes, adjusted the seat and mirrors, backed off the pier, and drove home to resume my life as if I'd never died.

Chapter Twelve

If you think the first thing I did was get a colorful Spandex costume made so I could fly around looking like I was wearing underwear and a cape, forget it. While God had pretty much left me on my own to generate a strategy to win back the earth for him, I didn't think looking like I was performing a circus act at a Las Vegas casino hotel was a good first step.

The job I had been given was to rally people already on our side and win supporters from the undecided and away from the opposition. I'd been hired by God as a publicist trying to sell a way of looking at things. If I'd started thinking of myself as some sort of savior, it wouldn't have been about the mission anymore; it would have been about me.

Don't get me wrong. I made careful calculations of exactly how much face time I could get on TV if I flew a couple of loop-de-loops in front of a Fox News camera crew, took a stroll on the surface of the Mississippi River with CNN taping, or pulled a real Superman stunt by rescuing people where even firemen thought it was impossible. But I didn't want to have to spend all my time breaking out of the locked cells doing stunts like this would have put me in, after investigators dispatched by everything from the Pentagon to the Centers for Disease Control and Prevention decided they needed to know what made me tick.

If my "super" powers were going to be of any use to me at all on this mission (and I wasn't at all certain they were) my use of them was going to have to be discreet, selective, and subtle. This wasn't a job for a superman so much as it was a job for a writer who could get published in a great metropolitan newspaper.

God had said a circle would form around me. But I didn't know who they were and when they would show up. In the meantime, I was on my own.

One important decision I had already made. I was not going to throw my own hat into the ring as the gubernatorial candidate of the Party of God. I had played back God's message to me several times and listened carefully to what he had told me. He had called me an ambassador and a campaign manager. He didn't say anything about my being a candidate, myself.

It looked as if my first job was to find a candidate whose campaign I could manage and convince him or her to run.

I had no idea how much support I could expect from existing churches, synagogues, and mosques. They all said they were on God's side but even if they really were, a proposition that didn't seem at all certain to me, why would any of them give me the time of day? If I just told them the truth about my mission, why wouldn't they consider me a heretic? If I performed a small miracle to convince them of my credentials, why wouldn't they regard me as a demon sent to deceive them?

Then there were all those people out there who weren't affiliated with any organized religion but who considered themselves "spiritual." It looked to me like this was already a saturated market, with a popular medium channeling ghosts on TV, an author writing about *his* conversations with God (I wondered if God had served him as good a breakfast), people looking for secret messages in the Bible, and a guy who repeatedly got struck by lightning trying to explain how the universe worked to people who didn't even know where their fuse box was.

No, if I was going to have to actively hunt for a candidate, I was going to have to find the right person the slow way, by looking into people's hearts, one by one, and seeing what was there.

Moreover the decision might also depend on who the Anorexics were going to run for governor. It seemed completely unlikely to me that Lucifer intended to run for the office herself. With the tunnels out of service until the end of the Interregnum, she wouldn't be able to campaign in person unless she'd moved headquarters to earth and was trapped here. With all three of the Trinity excluded from running, and Lucifer not in the race, it was likely that both parties were going to be running their candidate as a proxy.

At least I didn't have to worry about third-party candidates and independents entering the race. Lucifer was worried enough about the Party of God. The full text of Satan's treaty with God were in my briefing documents on my internal desktop, which included details of how the election was to be conducted. Lucifer had insisted, and God had conceded, that third-party candidates and independents wouldn't be on the ballot.

Too bad. On election day I might have crossed over party lines myself and voted Libertarian.

I realized that the first thing I needed to do was scope out the opposition camp, see who they might be thinking about running, and find out just exactly what I was up against.

Meanwhile, I still had my day job — four hours a day, five days a week — as a radio talk show host. I might not yet have been certain just exactly how I was going to accomplish my mission but I was pretty sure of two things. The first was that my ability to speak weekdays to a large radio audience was an asset. The second was that if I started talking too much on the air about theology, I'd lose my audience, my Arbitron rating, and my show, in that order.

I really shouldn't have worried so much. Things have a way of working out for themselves, when you're on a mission from God.

I was back in the K-TALK studios only a few days when my engineer, Terry, told me during an off-air break that I had a personal call. "You're not going to believe this," he told me, "but it's Manchu Ellins."

"Are you sure?" I asked him.

"Unless we have someone who can play around inside Pac Bell," Terry said. "That's how the caller ID comes up and I don't think it's Rich Little doing the voice."

I picked up the phone to see if the caller was indeed the legendary movie actor/director/producer whose last eight pictures had each grossed over three hundred million bucks. "Duj Pepperman," I said.

"Manchu Ellins," the voice said. It was him, all right.

The voice, the speech mannerisms, were unmistakable. "I didn't think you'd be surprised to be hearing from me. I thought you'd have been given some advance warning?"

"Look for a circle to form around you," God had told me, but the first in the circle was one of the half dozen people in Hollywood whose "yes" to a project was an automatic green light?

I could see Terry still listening in from the booth. I give him the signal that this was a private call. He looked disappointed but hung up his extension.

"Yes, Mr. Ellins," I said. "I didn't know that it was going to be from you specifically but I have been expecting a call."

"Good, that will save us some preliminaries," he said. "Would you allow me to show you my hospitality by coming by my house for dinner? Or if you prefer," he said with a little chuckle, "there are some nice clubs where I never seem to have a problem getting a good table."

"Your house will be fine," I said, trying to sound cool, when actually, there was a little kid inside of me jumping up and down. Meeting God was one thing, but this was a *movie* star.

"Do you have plans for this evening?" he asked.

"No other plans," I said. "I've been keeping my calendar loose."

"I'm at the house in Beverly Hills. I'll have my assistant fax you Yahoo directions, unless you'd prefer that I send a limousine?"

"That's very generous, but I like to drive," I told him.

"Cocktails at eight-thirty, dinner at nine. Don't

bother dressing for dinner; I'll be in shorts and a Lakers jersey," he said, then hung up.

Wow! I thought. This whole world-saving business might not be as hard as I'd worried. Manchu Ellins. Guest on *The Tonight Show* with a simple phone call. Name recognition surpassed only by Mickey Mouse. Ruggedly handsome, Best Actor Oscar for playing a hero in the War Against Terrorism, so iconoclastic that he had fans both on the left and the right.

The perfect candidate.

Terry saw me hang up the phone and opened up the studio intercom.

"You'll never believe whose house I'm having dinner at tonight," I told him.

Terry, who was impossible to impress, looked impressed. "Who did *you* fuck that you rate the A list?" he asked.

"It's not me, this is some business for our boss," I told him.

"If his wife is going to be there," Terry said, "I'm going to kill you and go in your place."

"Been there, done that," I said, grinning at him through the glass, and we barely made it back on the air in time after the traffic report was finished.

Chapter Thirteen

Let me tell you, there are options built into Body By Jesus that you never knew you were missing until you have them, and which you wonder how you'd ever be able to live without them once you do.

Take physical fitness, for example.

In the *corpus novus*, fitness has nothing to do with cosmetic appearance, which is in an entirely different menu. I could look fat or thin, young or old, bald as Yul Brynner or hairy as the '67 Beatles, fit as a fiddle or looking like I was on my last legs, and it had nothing to do with how I felt, how strong I was, what I ate, or whether I ever exercised.

I'd already activated a cosmetic dynamic I'd wished for in my old body: during the next twenty weeks my body was going to look two pounds of fat lighter, and a quarter pound of muscle more hard-bodied, each week. I was finally going to have those washboard abs I'd seen on late-night TV. I could have morphed my appearance in an instant, of course, but people would have talked.

But that had nothing at all to do with how "fit" I was.

My old body had only one ordinary means of generating the energy necessary for my life: absorbing external biomass into my own biomass, where I either burned it for energy, built cells, or stored it as fat for later use.

My new body can be set to convert and use as energy pretty much anything around me, whether it's electricity, background noise or left-over heat from a Big Bang, electromagnetic waves (sunlight, radio broadcasts), chemical (if it's matter, I can eat it and burn it), conventional nuclear (fission, fusion, anti-matter plasma), electrochemical-nuclear (cold fusion), or even — though it's on other menus—forces ranging from the space-time warping of ordinary gravity to an exploding supernova. Yes, I have a new set of extrasensory organs to taste each of these energies — and I have to tell you, music tastes a whole lot better than the noise of a garbage truck.

I don't know how you'd look at having this much power available at your beck and call, but if this isn't being made into a god, I don't know what is.

Final judgment before being resurrected isn't only about whether you're good or evil, although that's the first cut. It's also about whether you have the innate decency and self-control not to hog too much ambient energy for yourself or to misuse the power you keep and bear that can take out a galaxy if you get pissed off.

Simply being resurrected into the new body is the greatest compliment, the greatest statement of trust, anyone, anywhere, has ever paid you. It's like winning gold at the Olympics, the Congressional Medal of Honor, the Nobel Prize, and the Prometheus Award all rolled into one. It's the ultimate Oscar.

When I drove out of the K-TALK studios to Manchu Ellins' Beverly Hills estate for dinner, I was hungry.

I was hungry because I'd set the power defaults in my body only to use conventional food digestion as its energy source, except for some safety options to cut in automatically if I stepped on a land mine or was shot at. Yes, all the energy in the universe, and more, was there for me to eat in an all-you-can-eat buffet. But I had to regulate what I ate even more than when I was in my old body. The food was different but I still had to watch my intake carefully because it wasn't safe for an inexperienced god to walk around earth cocked and locked for universal calamity.

The Ellins mansion was hidden behind polished black walls that would have looked at home on an embassy, the *nouvelle mode* ever since the International Terrorist Network first targeted the entertainment industry. Inside the gate I noticed that a huge expanse that could have been the front lawn was instead a carefully maintained rock garden. Otherwise, the mansion looked like it could have been used for exteriors of Tara during filming of *Gone With The Wind*.

I couldn't help noticing the one car parked haphazardly in the driveway in front of the house. It was his McLaren F1 sports car, a racer equivalent in artistic value to a Stradivarius violin, which Ellins evidently drove out if he needed a pack of gum.

Ellins met me at the cavernous front door and invited me into his home with a warm two-handed shake.

The first thing I noticed about the interior of the house was that it looked as if a moving van was expected. The entrance hall led to a living room that was completely unfurnished: no furniture, nothing on the walls. The room next to that, looking as if it had been intended as a dining hall, was instead outfitted as a fitness center with stair climbers, stationery bikes, weight machines, rowers, and treadmills. There was also a bench with a set of free weights off to the side.

In person, Manchu Ellins projected the same good-natured self-confidence that had won him the People's Choice award six-years-running. He had his trademark two-day beard and obviously used the fitness equipment; for a man pushing sixty he still had the lean muscle masses and smooth skin of a man half his age.

Almost without thinking, I automatically stripped away his temporal presence and started checking out his inner self, when he placed a hand on my arm, stopping me. He'd caught me out. "Now *that*'s not very polite," he said, smiling. "How would you feel if the first thing I did was undress *your* soul?"

"Sorry, it's gotten to be a habit," I said, embarrassed.

"No sweat," he said. "Would you like a drink, Your Excellency?"

I was a little taken aback. I knew God had named me his ambassador, but this was the first time I'd encountered anyone else who knew it and I'd certainly had no expectation of being addressed with formal protocol.

I tried to let it slide. "Sure."

"Anything in particular?"

"Whatever you're having," I said.

"Come on, I've got just the thing."

Instead of leading me to a bar, Ellins led me into a kitchen with a huge wooden butcher block in the center. It was completely covered with what looked to be vitamins, minerals, herbs, and food supplements. Again, there were no tables or chairs but it looked as if all the countertop appliances had arrived.

"How long have you had this house?" I asked, trying to sound casual.

"Oh, let's see," he said, a bit distracted. He was pulling various smoke-colored bottles out of the refrigerator and pouring from them into a drink mixer of the sort you'd find in an old fashioned soda fountain. "Seven, no, eight years. Lynnie and I moved in here right after her first miscarriage."

"Lynnie" was his gorgeous wife, Caulinn Helms, lead singer of the grunge band Seminal Lunch, and the cause of my engineer's adolescent attack of drool. "I'm sorry I asked," I said. "I didn't mean to bring up painful memories."

"It's not painful anymore. We've come to realize becoming parents was just a bad idea anyway."

He ran the mixer a bit, pulled two huge frosted glasses from a compartment of his freezer, then filled them and handed me one. "Your health," he said, clinking my glass with his.

"Yours too," I said, and took a sip.

I don't know what it was. I've tried hard to eliminate that memory. It had the texture of chalk, the taste of mold, and the smell of used socks.

"Ahhhhhhhhh!" he said, downing the whole glass in one gulp.

He saw my expression and laughed. "I guess it is an acquired taste," he said. "Come on, I want you to meet my wife."

He led me up a spiral staircase, taking the stairs

two at a time, until we came to the master bedroom
… or whatever you called a sleeping room that had
no bed or any other furniture. Caulinn Helms was sitting with her legs splayed wide open on a weaved mat,
reading a book titled *The Myth of Gender*. She was
completely naked, and aside from the silky black hair
on her head, she was completely shaved.

I immediately felt the utility of my *not* being naked.

"Darling," Ellins said to his wife, "this is His Excellency Duj Pepperman, Ambassador from the Celestial Palace and Terrestrial Coordinator of the Party of
God."

Caulinn Helms stood up, came so close to me I could
smell her sex, and took my hand. "I'm delighted to
meet you, Ambassador," she said in that low whiskey
voice of hers. There was nothing shy about her; she
immediately looked down to my crotch. "And I can
see that you're delighted to meet me, too," she said.

I don't think I have ever been so thoroughly aroused,
embarrassed, and bewildered, all at the same time. If
I'd been in private I would have called up a menu and
turned off my libido for the duration of this visit, but I
never got the chance.

Neither of them seemed to be aware of my discom-
fort. I concluded her household nudity was so com-
monplace that they didn't even notice it anymore.

"Would you like a tour of the house before dinner?"
she asked. She dropped her book on the floor, not
worrying if she lost her page, and bounded down the
spiral staircase, ahead of us.

"She's really quite a piece of ass, isn't she?" Ellins
said to me, as we descended the staircase at a more

stately pace. "There's no mystery why every man on earth, and half the women, want to fuck her."

All I could do was nod while steadying myself using the banister on the way down.

Yes, they're real.

A complete discussion of her surgeries, her abortions, and how she had done away with the necessity for bowel movements by regular use of high colonics, was served along with dinner, but it was a party that I think even Lewis Carroll would have had a hard time imagining.

Dinner was served on the hardwood floor in the living room. Manchu and Caulinn each sat cross-legged in Lotus, he in his basketball shorts and jersey, she still completely nude, with the food dishes set in front of us. My new body was limber enough to get into the position but it took some effort to avoid falling over.

I asked them about the lack of furniture in their house, now that I knew it was intended. "We don't believe in furniture," Caulinn explained. "The human body just wasn't designed for it."

It wasn't just furniture that was missing from their house. An Olympic-sized swimming pool behind the house was drained. There wasn't a TV set, radio, stereo, or musical instrument anywhere in the house. I saw no magazines, no sculptures, paintings, family photos, or other artistic installations, and neither was there any other sort of interior decoration.

I'd seen prison cells that were better furnished.

There were extensive built-in bookshelves but no

books on them; in fact, the only other book I saw anywhere in the house was in the kitchen, a piece of light
reading titled, *A Guide to Marine Coastal Plankton and
Marine Invertebrate Larvae.*

Which brings us back to dinner. "We're not vegetar-
ians," Manchu explained. "We simply believe in eating as low on the food chain as possible."

I believe they had reached the bottom. Dinner that
night was sushi made with reconstituted freeze-dried
plankton and fresh frozen Antarctic krill.

During this feast, while Manchu Ellins lectured me
on the indisputable scientific evidence proving that
the dangerously expanding hole in the ozone layer
was caused by second-hand tobacco smoke, Caulinn
started gently caressing her nipples, arousing herself.
That naturally brought the dinner discussion back to
the topic of sex.

I tried to stay nonchalant about her erotic behavior.
I was in their house, after all, with their customs, and
this was not a public display.

"When Manny and I met," Caulinn told me, "we
were both bisexual and very active, but after we got
married we decided that being gay just wasn't enough.
It just wasn't the statement we wanted to make."

"Well, I can easily understand that," I said. "Both of
you are at your physical peak with good looks and
maximum appeal. It's obvious that you love each other.
I'm sure you realize that fantasies about your sex life
together make you envied by millions."

"Oh, we haven't had sex in years," Caulinn explained. "With each other or anybody else. We've both
taken vows of chastity."

I don't think I allowed my jaw to drop.

"As for physical fitness," Caulinn continued, "we don't do it because we like it. Looking a certain way is just a necessity for keeping our box office revenues up."

"Don't you think it's time we got down to business, dear?" Manchu Ellins said to his wife. "I'm sure the ambassador doesn't want to listen to us talking shop all night."

He turned to me. "I take it, Ambassador, that you haven't yet selected a candidate to represent the Party of God in the upcoming election?"

I was still more than a bit distracted. Caulinn had dropped her hand between her legs and was massaging her vulva.

Manchu saw my expression. "Oh, don't mind her," he said. "Masturbation is the only sexual release we allow ourselves. We just do it whenever the urge strikes."

"It's very healthy," Caulinn said. "And veeery relaxing. I can see you're aroused. I won't mind at all if you decide to masturbate with me."

I knew that my engineer, Terry, would have given up a kidney for this opportunity, but I suddenly managed to put it all together, and pulled myself out of the tailspin I was in.

"No, Mr. Ellins," I said. "I haven't yet made that decision. I'll send you formal notification before the filing deadline. Are you the gubernatorial candidate of the Anorexic Party, or will it be your wife?"

"I'll be running," said Ellins.

I could see that Caulinn Helms was getting near to

orgasm. With some difficulty I rose to my feet.

Manchu Ellins' attention wasn't on me anymore; he was now rubbing his own genitals through his shorts. It was obvious that the business portion of the evening was already over.

"Thank you for your hospitality," I said, not sure either of them was listening to me any more. "No, don't bother getting up. I'll let myself out."

I walked outside to my Mercedes, drove out the gate, and was halfway back to Culver City when I felt like an idiot. Damn!

I'd forgotten to get their autographs.

Chapter Fourteen

The days when human beings had any common understanding about the origins and nature of their lives were buried deep in human prehistory.

Ever since the fall of Eden, and the catastrophic events that followed, human beings began to disagree with each other about who we were, where we came from, why we were here, and what it all meant. Get three human beings together and you had eight different opinions on these questions.

Even after the last of the first angelic colonists had returned to the celestial realm, religious and political events on earth were still being closely affected by heavenly interventions, most of them chronicled by human reporters, with widely varying degrees of accuracy, in those texts that human beings call their holy scriptures.

But within a few centuries after Jesus lived and died on earth, so many human communities were isolated, so many important books had been destroyed by intolerance and war, so much religious and political strife had fractured common language, that there was simply no human consensus by which communiqués from God to the human race could be universally understood.

The Celestial Agreement of Terrestrial Interregnum that began with the Christian Reformation was both a curse and a blessing for the human race.

The bad news was that with the tunnels between

Heaven and earth closed, and access to the Tree of Knowledge shut off, we were pretty much on our own to sink or swim.

The good news was that deprived of any centrally respected authority to dictate what was true and what wasn't, human exploration was free to flower, and the civilizations we built, based on our natural philosophies and sciences, proved that we did indeed have the spark of God still alive in us.

While the worst of us were still hung up on figuring out innovative ways to ruin the lives of our perceived enemies, the best of us were teaching the whole world how to capitalize our way out of abject poverty, fly to the moon and claim it for all mankind, and create an Internet that made sharing knowledge among ourselves almost as universal to the developed world as the Tree of Knowledge itself.

Unfortunately, as widespread as the Internet grew in the early twenty-first century, there were still vast continents where it was unknown. And the problem of how to hold an election on earth, where all humanity could vote, was a problem that Lucifer and her minions didn't know how to solve for themselves when Lucifer demanded of God that an election determine who would rule earth.

There were nations that decided things by elections, sure, but there were as many people residing where rulership was by one party and few if anyone even had a clue what an election looked like. Moreover, the Interregnum's imposition of heavenly embargo and mass invincible ignorance had left many of those in positions of power unaware that earth's extraterritoriality was even up for grabs.

Communicating this simple fact, obscured for close to half a millennium, to billions of souls on earth, was a formidable enough problem. Explaining to human beings that of all their religious faiths only prophetic writings from one even referenced the cast of characters involved in this dispute, though misidentifying the means by which the conflict was to be resolved, was even more daunting.

St. John the Divine had correctly understood from his prophetic dreams that the outcome of a civil war in Heaven would also determine the fate of earth, but that's about the only thing he got right. He didn't know how to read a celestial calendar, he didn't understand how the tunnels worked, and he didn't have the diplomatic education to understand the treaty ending that war, which provided for an orderly transition of power. It's hard enough to write history with any degree of accuracy. Trying to describe events in a future you don't understand is pretty much impossible. Sorry to have disappointed those of you grooving in anticipation of the Rapture, the Battle of Armageddon and the Four Horsemen of the Apocalypse.

Even worse for Lucifer and the Anorexic Party, their hatred for everything invented, including technology, left them as a group still pretty much "computer illiterate," as Jesus had put it to me. Outright rejecting use of the Tree as a means of counting eligible voters much less votes, and not trusting independent consultants who understood a technology they didn't, they had no solution of their own on how to reacquaint the people of earth with their history, communicate to them the issues at stake, and poll their decisions.

That was why Lucifer had looked so diminished at her first official press conference, when she'd announced the Anorexic Party victory. She'd had to swallow her pride and ask God to solve the problem of how to hold the election on earth. She was like a rebellious teenager who'd decided to move into her own place who had just discovered she needed to borrow her dad's van for the move.

God could have simply done nothing and things on earth could have remained as they were, with human beings running their own affairs, as greatly and terribly as we usually do.

Perhaps we might have avoided destroying our technological civilization long enough to expand our race out to other solar systems, and even outlived the death of our own life-sustaining sun, but eventually our universe itself would have ended, and with God having signed a treaty that neither he nor his loyalists would interfere, that would have been it for us.

Twenty billion or so years until the end of a universe might seem a long time for you and me, because we are so young. But for God, who has seen universes come and go like the seasons, it would be a loss of many beloved grandchildren that he could anticipate and dread.

As always, God was not about to give up. He gave Lucifer the solution she had asked for, and the election to determine the destiny of the human race was on.

Human beings spoke thousands of different languages. We had hundreds of different faiths and some of us had no faith. Many of us were illiterate. Some of us were newborn on earth and some of us had once again been trapped into reincarnating here during the Interregnum, roaming the earth as ghosts in between lives, as in the days before the tender of salvation.

God's solution to the problem of human diversity was elegant.

We all still dreamed.

It was in dreams that we would learn of earth's origins and the origins of our species. It was in dreams that we would be told, in symbols each of us could understand, what the platforms were of each party and how we could cast our vote. And it was in dreams, on a single day and night, that each of us would cast our vote for the fate of our birthland and of our species.

On our first awakening after the election, those of us living would remember our dream with perfect clarity, and learn that all of us had experienced the same dream.

The results of the election would be the last thing we were told before we awoke.

Well, that's the way the whole thing was supposed to work, anyway.

A few weeks after my dinner with the Anorexic candidate and his wife, I was still wondering who on earth was in my own party.

Back in my college days, you could always tell the real leadership of any campus political organization. It wasn't necessarily the person who carried the title of "president," "coordinator, "chair," or even "secretary." The leadership was whoever held the funds, and whoever had the membership list.

I hadn't been given so much as a Party of God Christmas card list, and if there was a bank account somewhere with that name on it, I wasn't a signatory. In fact, the only Party of God I could even find a reference to on the Internet was a Palestinian guerrilla group that had fallen into complete obscurity a couple of years after Israel became the 56th state in the union.

I don't know what I was thinking. God doesn't need money. And he doesn't need any stinking mailing lists.

I was alone in my living room, learning some new physical options that came with my resurrection, when a ghost walked into the room. Well, he wasn't really a ghost; he was a resurrected human maintaining his mass at about one percent, which made him able to pass through walls but not quite invisible. He looked familiar to me, but I couldn't place him right away.

He was a bit taller than medium height, military trim, looked in his late twenties or early thirties, and he had the physical presence of a silent-film-era matinee idol, with slick dark hair, a handsome face, and a dapper mustache.

He increased his mass to earth normal so I could see him in color. He was wearing sharply creased white trousers, spit-shined white shoes, a creme ascot, and a purple velvet smoking jacket—which was appropriate since he was smoking a cigarette held in a long cigarette holder.

He gave a little wink and saluted me. "Permission to come aboard, sir?" he asked, with a slight Southern lilt to his voice.

I chopped my hand to my forehead. "We're on land,

friend, but permission granted anyway. Who are you?"

"The Ghost of Christmas Future," he said with a big smile.

It was then I recognized him. He looked about fifty years younger than the last time I'd seen him, while giving blood at a science-fiction convention.

It was Robert A. Heinlein.

Do you remember how I explained earlier in this narrative how some human beings originated as angels who incarnated as human to learn how to dream so they could advance to godhood, while others were souls originating on earth who became gods when resurrected?

You might have already guessed that some of the greatest human beings in history started their lives as angels. You already know a lot of their traveling names: Socrates, Buddha, Confucius, Joan, Mozart, Gandhi, Pocahontas, Douglass, Michelangelo, Smith.

But some of the greatest of our tribe were home-grown: David, Mohammed, Aesop, Da Vinci, Wollstonecraft, Beethoven, Edison, Jefferson, Disney, Smith.

Robert A. Heinlein was one of our luminaries, but he was no angel.

As a genre of literature, science fiction's greatest contributions have not been characters or style, but images and thoughts. This has left it often neglected by the unimaginative and the thoughtless. It is the how-to literature of creation, the craft of awakened dreams.

Robert A. Heinlein is known in Heaven as one of the human race's greatest dreamers.

"Mind if I smoke?" he asked me.

"The last time I answered that question," I replied, "my life changed forever."

"I promise this will do nothing dry cleaning can't handle," he said.

"Then feel free," I told him. "By the way, do you happen to know what happens to people who object to Jesus' smoking?"

"They go right to hell," he joked, chuckling in a way that reminded me of a buzzsaw.

"Please, Mr. Heinlein, make yourself comfortable," I told him.

"Bob," he said, settling into an armchair.

"Duj," I offered back. "Can I get you something to eat?"

"No thank you. Ginny and I just finished dinner a short while ago."

"A cognac then?"

"Can you make it a B and B over ice?" he asked.

I poured us each a bourbon and brandy and handed him one.

He toasted,

> "Here's to them that sail to sea
> And the ladies that stay on land.
> May the former be well rigged
> And the latter be well manned!"

We clinked glasses and drank. I didn't even have to peep him. No way this renowned sybarite was a member of the Anorexic Party, even if he had been an agnostic while alive.

"I was told a circle would form," I told him. "Can I assume you're the first of our political party to make an appearance?"

"The Central Committee has already been called up and the Chairman Pro Tem is waiting right now for you to take his seat," he told me.

"Thank God," I said. "I've been waiting for the other shoe to drop ever since I got back. Do we leave right now?"

"President Jefferson would expect us not to waste our drinks," he said.

This was going to be fun. "Where's the meeting?"

He raised an eyebrow. "I happen to know that you've familiarized yourself with my tall tales," he said. "Why don't you tell *me* where the meetings are always held?"

I thought for a moment. "You're kidding me. 'Lost Legacy'? The summit of Mount Shasta?"

He smiled, draining his drink and standing up. "Ready to fly?"

Chapter Fifteen

There's just no other way to put it. Heinlein is a show-off.

It was about a 600-mile flight north from Culver City to Mount Shasta. Since this was my first flight since I had returned to earth, I was happy simply to look down at the California scenery, past the Grapevine, over Pea Soup Anderson's, past farmland and rolling hills, around Sacramento, until, from about 100 miles away, Mount Shasta came into view.

I was flying pretty much level and steady. Meanwhile, Heinlein was doing aerobatics: barrel rolls, eight-point rolls, the back stroke, full loops, and just for variety, an occasional quadruple gainer with two-and-a-half twists. I felt like shouting at him, "Orange wings! Be careful or the flightmaster will ground you!" but wasn't sure how well he'd remember his own stories and whether he'd get the inside joke. We made good time anyway, and the flight was less than an hour.

In case you were about to cluck your tongue about our drinking and flying, keep in mind that our resurrected bodies could handle drinking Love Canal without being affected.

Weather on the summit was mild for Mount Shasta when we dropped in for our landing. The Great Assembly Hall, like Mount Shasta itself, was built like a pyramid, but was a layer off dimension so it wouldn't be perceptible to mortals. Heinlein and I walked inside.

The Central Committee of the Party of God has no decision-making authority of its own. It exists as an advisory body, a cabinet, for God's designated hitter. There were no permanent seats on it; it was more or less like a minion in Jewish law or a jury pool in American courts. Whoever qualified that was around when the Coordinator needed help was pulled in for service.

The qualifications for the jury pool were particularly lofty, and a bunch of really accomplished people had volunteered to trap themselves on earth until the gates reopened to help me prepare for the election. Angels were not permitted to serve on the committee, not even angels who had incarnated as human. Eligibility required being a resurrected native-born earthling.

Since this was the first time I was being presented to them, they made it into a show. Aside from Heinlein and myself there were fifteen delegates in attendance, queued up in a reception line. But the fifteen standing before me represented not only their most recent incarnations, but also some of the most memorable personages in human history.

They all applauded as I entered, then Heinlein guided me down the line, making formal introductions. I took the opportunity to exchange a few personal words with each one who seemed amenable to it.

"Saul Ben-Samuel Pepperman," he said, using my real first name and my father's, "may I present to you the Chairman Pro Tem, Thomas Jefferson *née* King Solomon ..."

"The Declaration of Independence is the single best piece of writing in human history, sir," I told him.

"Henry Louis Mencken *née* Benjamin Franklin."

"Mr. Franklin, I agree about not deserving liberty, but how do we make men brave?"

"Goldie Mabovitch *née* Elizabeth Regina."

"Mrs. Meir, my grandmother once told me you gave a speech in her living room."

"William Claude Dukenfield *née* Aristophanes."

"This sure beats Philadelphia, doesn't it?"

"Sheikh Mushariff-Ud-Din Sa'di."

"*Khosh amadid.*"

"Alissa Rosenbaum *née* Aristotle."

"The way I would phrase that, Miss Rand, is 'either-ornery.'"

"Clive Staples Lewis *née* Durante Alighieri."

"So on November 22nd, 1963, you, Jack Kennedy, and Aldous Huxley all met just outside the tunnel and decided to go pub hopping together?"

"George Bernard Shaw."

"How are you handling immortality?"

"Raymond William Stacy Burr *née* Aaron Burr."

"Nice shot," I said.

"Samuel Langhorne Clemens."

"Did you ever find out what happened to your friend Mr. Bierce?"

"Martin Luther King, Jr., *née* Martin Luther."

"You just took that reincarnation because you wanted to keep your old name?"

"Norma Jean Baker *née* Cleopatra."

"You know, you remind me so much of a close friend of mine named Estella."

"George Smith Patton, Jr., *née* Alexander the Great."

"I would have gone on to finish off Stalin, too."

"Charles Augustus Lindbergh *née* Meriwether Lewis *née* Marco Polo."

"The violin originated not in Italy but in China?"

"Ludwig von Mises *née* Adam Smith."

"So you've completed the first draft of *Deistic Action*?"

After introductions, we removed into the conference room, seating ourselves at a round table of the same sort I'd encountered at breakfast with God: floating midair with self-positioning chairs. But this table was a lot bigger.

President Jefferson as Chairman Pro Tem gaveled the meeting to order, welcomed me again, then turned the meeting over to me.

"Thank you, Mr. President," I said. "This is new to me. Do you mind acting as parliamentarian for me? Advise me regarding rules of order?"

"That will be easy, sir," Jefferson said. "This is your meeting. Each of us will speak only when you ask for one of us to do so."

"There is no set agenda? No old business?"

"None."

Okay. Try to put yourself in my place for a second. You're in a room with sixteen of the most brilliant, most famous, most accomplished human beings of your race, people who *are* human history, and the one whom the rest of them have decided is perhaps the smartest and most accomplished of the lot has just told you they're waiting to find out what you want to do.

How did I get picked for this job? I wondered. Just because God gave me a long swim in his gene pool, did that make me qualified even to sit among these giants, much less lead them?

I looked over to Jefferson again and saw him smiling. I knew that he had been exactly where I was sitting and knew exactly how I felt.

I had to start somewhere and picked one almost at random.

"General Patton, I was under the impression that we faced a political engagement with the opposition, not a military one. Are you here to advise me in your professional capacity as a military man, or elsewise?"

"I'm here in case the enemy acts true to form," Patton said. "They don't play by the rules. You have to watch them like a hawk. You can't assume anything. You have to figure out where they're going and be there waiting for them."

"Do you expect we'll have to meet them in battle?"

"For once someone is asking my opinion *before* it's too late," Patton said. "We can't win this war by attacking the enemy through force."

"If you don't think so, general, I have no doubt it's true."

He nodded and went on. "But they might contemplate using force against our positions to disrupt our operations. With proper preparations, we can foreclose the force option to the enemy before they can use it."

"You've foreseen such preparations? You have the logistical resources to carry them out?"

"I have, sir."

I spoke to the assembled others. "Is there anyone here who thinks they have a better take on the military sciences than General Patton?"

No one spoke up.

"Okay, then. General, please make a short, plain English executive summary of what security precautions you have in mind available to me at your earliest convenience. I'll review it and if it meets with my approval, I'll give you the command authority to carry it out."

"Yes, sir. You'll have it on your desktop within twenty-four hours."

I started relaxing. These people had my back.

"Who here can tell me what the Anorexic Party wants to achieve?"

"I can," said Ayn Rand.

"Please proceed, madam."

"They wish for veto power over all existence but they have only the power to destroy that we, ourselves, give them."

"Then you are critical of the Lord's decision to enable the election Lucifer demanded?"

"I wouldn't presume," she said, with her Russian accent coming back for a moment. "In this last life I searched for a real John Galt, a man smarter and more determined than I was to win all that was good from the world. I had a lot of dreams, but I never dreamt that I would meet him in another world after I died. If God is offering them something they want, I must assume it is the cheese in a mouse trap."

"Is there anyone in the opposition camp smart enough to see that also?" I asked the table.

"Satan is quite clever enough for that," said C.S. Lewis. "I think Alexander—excuse me, sir—I mean General Patton, will agree with me that Satan is a strategic genius."

"Perhaps," I said, "but we've read her book, haven't we, General?"

That got me a laugh, with Patton laughing the loudest. He was most famous for having outmaneuvered the German general, Rommel, in World War Two, because Patton had read Rommel's own book on tank warfare.

"But you don't win wars mainly with strategy," said Patton. "You win them with logistics, and more importantly, by putting men with guts into the field."

"You're politely suggesting to me, General, "that I should be concentrating on the question of who our candidate is going to be?"

"I've never been accused of being polite before, sir, but yes."

Patton had gotten the second laugh.

"I'm actually going in that direction, General," I said. "To know the right candidate, I need to know what to expect."

"You can expect mass disruptions," said Golda Meir. "Terrorism. Riots. Fires. Earthquakes. Volcanic eruptions. Every sort of destructive storm."

"And," added H.L. Mencken, "the biggest religious revival in human history."

"I can understand the spitefulness that would lead to random destruction," I said, "but I'm afraid you've lost me why Satan would want a religious revival. I thought that plays right into our strengths?"

"You can't underestimate the subtlety of Satan's planning," said the Sufi master, Sa'di of Shiraz.

"You must look at the Luciferian strategy from the standpoint of games theory," said Ludwig von Mises.

"The children of earth no longer routinely think of God, or of Satan, as real," said C.S. Lewis. "For most people religion is a ritual, or a social occasion, or a safe haven for their children. It is only in fear or grief, confronting mortality and the beyond that has been hidden from them, that they pay any serious mind to their hopes that the old stories are true and that there is the hope of salvation for them."

"Look at what holiday gains more prominence every year," said Mark Twain. "Is it Christmas? No, that has become a shopping expedition—no offense to you, Mr. Polo."

"None taken."

"Nor," continued Lewis, "is it Easter, the day meant to remind us of the good news."

"And it's certainly not my birthday," said Dr. King with a smile.

"We're not trying to keep you guessing. We're talking about Halloween," said H.L. Mencken.

Ayn Rand said, "Life is a suspense story. What makes it suspenseful is not knowing how it comes out."

"The biggest mystery," said Raymond Burr, "the one that has people lying in bed awake at night — is whether or not you die when your body dies. All you know when you're on Earth is life within your frail body. It is difficult to imagine living without it."

"The evidence of the senses is not enough to tell you what you really are, said Lewis. "Science tells you that you're a biochemical reaction trapped in a piece of meat, and when you die, the reaction fizzles and the meat rots. Most of the frightful symbols of death relate to dead bodies in various states of disintegration: skulls, bones, meat lockers, graves, and the paraphernalia of the undertaker. If that isn't enough, horror stories try to make it worse with three awful ideas: first that this rotting meat is all that's left of you when you die; second and worse: that after you die you're a disembodied ghost trapped in post-life impotence; or third and worst: that you're still conscious inside the rotting meat, and can experience the slow rotting."

Rand said, "Halloween goblins are promoted by people who wish to frighten us and reap the benefits of that fear."

"That was the purpose of Satan's demand for an Interregnum," said the blonde bombshell who'd previously been the original Queen of the Nile. "To give generations time to forget the world to come."

"It's a confidence game and," said Twain, with a twinkle in his eye, "you're the mark. If mortal men knew down deep, without doubt, that we were going to continue living once we separate from the flesh — and not forever as ghosts, either — our fear couldn't be used to stampede us."

"But," I asked, "why would Lucifer wish to stampede us into the arms of God?"

"Not into the arms of the Lord," said Martin Luther King. "The children of earth are told to flock to churches where God may listen ... but where the Lord's voice has been silenced, and his hand stilled. People pray until their lips are dry ... and they hear nothing back. The Lord cannot rescue them because his children are held hostage. The enemy is free to say, 'You see? Do you see? The Lord had the power to save you from this ... yet he did nothing. The Lord will do nothing next time. The Lord doesn't care for you.'"

"So," I said, thinking aloud, "in order to get people to join in her hatred of God, Lucifer must first get them to believe in God?"

"Just so," said C.S. Lewis. "But not belief in the God we know to be a loving father, a redeemer, a loving spirit. God is locked outside then we are told he is so indifferent to us that he won't lift a finger to help us. The victims begin seeing their kidnappers as their only friends. After my time it become known as the Stockholm syndrome."

"How diabolical," I said. I turned to Ayn Rand again. "I remember in your writings you always warned about the sanction of the victim."

"Yes?"

"Suppose we remove that sanction?"

"Just how do you suggest that we 'shrug'?" she asked. "Satan's only desire is annihilation. She is in favor of starvation already. Going on strike deprives her of nothing she needs and I am unaware of any way to escape from her prison other than winning an election it appears she has already fixed."

"Suppose we just play defense?" I asked.

"That only delays the inevitable," said Heinlein. "Ask General Patton about logistics. When an enemy is waging a war of attrition, one's only hope is to crack through their lines while you still can."

"Not," I said, surprising even myself at my boldness, "if left to their own devices the enemy will destroy themselves in time."

"Satan has set the calendar for these events," Jefferson reminded me. "Time is not on our side."

I turned to Mencken-Franklin. "As Franklin, you were a diplomat, yes?" I asked. He nodded. "You've studied the treaty?"

"Yes."

"Don't bother looking for loopholes," said W.C. Fields. "Satan already has all the best lawyers."

The laughter brought down the tension a bit.

"Well, I've read it, too," I said. "Mr. Franklin—and I am pointedly asking this on the basis of your previous incarnation—does or does not the treaty constrain me as tightly as God himself in performing miracles?"

He morphed into his previous incarnation. "The restriction on miracles applies to each of us as much as it applies to God," Benjamin Franklin explained.

"And that restriction is, precisely?"

"No miracles above π on the Aquinas Scale at any moment before the election. And none at all afterwards, if we lose."

"Well, how much of a miracle does that permit us?"

"The phrase 'π on the Aquinas Scale' is a term of art," said Raymond Burr, "referring to a miracle with the power to save one human life."

I cocked my head at him. "I may not have been a lawyer for a few hundred years, but more recently I played one on TV."

Everyone laughed again.

"Let's say that an airplane is about to crash with

over one hundred passengers," explained Franklin. "Since the limitation of π is the value of a single human life, God would be allowed to save only one of the passengers in that crash."

"And that treaty limitation would equally apply to each of us as well?"

"That is correct."

"How big a miracle would 10π be?" I asked.

"Strong enough a miracle to save Southern California from the Big One. The Aquinas scale is logarithmic."

"And if ten of us got into a daisy chain, could we, under the precise terms of the treaty with Satan, produce a miracle the power of 10π on the Aquinas scale?"

There was a stir in the room.

"By Jove," said Shaw, "I believe he has something."

"Will you indulge a few of us for several moments?" Jefferson asked.

I nodded.

Jefferson, Franklin, and Burr huddled for about two minutes, then returned to their seats.

The U.S. president formerly known as Solomon said, "I believe the treaty could reasonably and justly be interpreted as permitting that."

"That's good enough legal counsel for me," I said. "Ladies and gentlemen, the greater part of our task is now clear. We play defense. We calm the earth's tectonic plates, cool volcanoes, untwist twisters, and keep thugs with box cutters away from dangerous assets. With no mass misery to make political hay out of, the Anorexic Party will be unable to turn victims into voters."

"But who will be our standard bearer in the election?" Patton asked. "Who is the gubernatorial candidate for the Party of God?"

"Nobody," I said.

"What?"

"Nobody."

I could see Heinlein, Mencken, Twain, and Fields smiling. They'd already got it.

"You can't be serious," Golda Meir said.

"Look," I asked, "what was it God said? 'Resist not evil.' I've never been a pacifist. I'd love a good conventional war with these bozos. But think about it. They have nothing of their own as a platform, other than denial of pleasure, denial of creativity, denial of their own nature. They want to make God look indifferent to suffering while they make a big show out of looking compassionate. But they can only do that if we give them a target to shoot at.

"I say we give the Anorexics the very absence they wish from us, and give it to them now. We use our powers to stop their attacks on earth but that's all we do. We decline all debates. We don't campaign. We never even admit that God or Heaven exists or that there even exists a Party of God. Let people have the nightmares they'll give them then wake up and thank God it wasn't real.

"We don't have to win this election in order for the Interregnum to end and for the tunnels to the Celestial Palace to be opened up again. We simply have to let the Anorexic Party's candidate be rejected by the people of earth. Deprived of victims, they are out of business and free to look only to each other for the nothingness they have so richly earned.

"I will inform the Anorexic Party that we consent to their first proposed date for the election but that we will be assigning our ballot line to *None of the Above*. We reserve the right to edit out any untruthful, inaccurate or unbalanced statement they wish to make within their dream campaign, but we will make no arguments of our own.

"Under the terms of the treaty, any vote total less than fifty percent plus one fails the majority test necessary to rule the earth and earth will remain under the self rule of its people with one crucial difference: God's muzzle will be off for good.

"Upon the end of the Interregnum, we reveal ourselves. The tunnels to New Heaven will be open for two-way traffic. The Tree of Knowledge will be accessible through the Internet or from any public library. People on earth will be able to pray to God for any miracle they want with the rational expectation of benevolent response. And guided tours to visit New Heaven, using their astral bodies, will be available to any living human, death no longer a precondition of entry.

"Nobody is our candidate. Nobody in this election can be trusted with your future. Nobody on the ballot will keep his campaign promises. Vote for Nobody."

Sixteen of the greatest people in history rose to their feet and cheered me, this time with more than formal courtesy.

I was getting the idea that God knew me a whole lot better than I did.

Chapter Sixteen

A short digression.

I've had to make choices in this narrative about what I thought was important to bring up and what I should leave out. By way of full disclosure, I have to admit that I've allowed the entertainment instincts I developed on radio to guide me in those selections as much as, or more than, anything else.

For example, I haven't told you about any other family member than my daughter. I haven't mentioned many of my personal friends. I've told you practically nothing about my ex-wife.

Part of this is by their choice. Some of my friends and relatives actively campaigned for the Anorexic Party and asked me to leave them out of this narrative if I could. I also haven't wanted to burden you with aspects of my personal life that I just don't think are interesting to many people.

But I realize you might have thought it curious that, in particular, I haven't said anything about my parents, or whether I have any brothers or sisters. You might have come to the conclusion, from what God had said about cloning me, and from what Lucifer had said about God being Dr. Frankenstein, that my origins might have been in a Petrie dish rather than in a womb.

Put that thought out of your head. God doesn't need to work that way. In the ordinary course of human reproduction God has the power to effect very small miracles on gametes and zygotes when he needs them. I was born the usual way from ordinary human parents just like most of you were, not whipped up in some laboratory.

My parents were both alive at the time the events of this story took place, and living quite comfortably in a retirement community in Florida. I talked to them on the phone once or twice a week, and my dad, a retired cardiologist, played golf and sent me jokes in email. My mom, a retired ER triage nurse, played bridge, and loved TV game shows. They had just celebrated their 51st wedding anniversary.

I have no sisters and only one brother. He's got a doctorate from MIT in nuclear physics, was happily married with three kids, and at the time of these events was working at the Los Alamos National Laboratories on classified work he couldn't talk about.

If you got the idea that the reason I haven't mentioned other family and friends, when I talked about my time in Heaven, is that they hadn't made the cut, that's not it. There have been other pleasant times when we've caught up with each other again. Otherwise, let's just leave it that there are matters which are the private business of other people, and it's not my place to tell.

Before we adjourned, I placed General Patton in charge of calling up the militia — loyalist saved humans, earthbound angels, and even ghosts between incarnations — to serve as the Home Guard. Patton, in turn, delegated the job of Chief of Intelligence to the former Aaron Burr, not only because Burr was a master of intrigue, but also because he best knew how to use ghosts as intelligence operatives.

Burr's second-in-command was the former Queen of Egypt, known for some intrigues herself, and I wondered whether there would be any romance between these two actors, considering Burr's sexual preference in his last incarnation. But if any woman could turn a gay man straight again, Marilyn Monroe was definitely the one.

More than half the committee were renowned as writers. While the campaign strategy didn't call for any agit-prop, never underestimate the continuing necessity of preaching to the choir. We were also going to need ongoing analysis of the opposition camp's propaganda, and the development of effective counters.

I picked Thomas Jefferson/King Solomon as my attorney general, Heinlein as my chief of staff, H.L. Mencken/Benjamin Franklin as my press secretary (we wouldn't be talking to mortals, but there were millions of others who'd be following the campaign) and Martin Luther/King as my Deputy Consul. He was going to have the fun of telling the Anorexic Party that we were calling their bluff, and it was his job to tell me how they took it. I figured that a man who was intimidated by neither pope nor klansman would be able to remain steady, no matter what curve they threw him.

I had a very special solo assignment for Lindbergh/Lewis/Polo, which I'll get to later.

As for me, it was my intention to put the right people into the right jobs and stay out of their way.

I gave everyone present my unlisted number and went home.

Martin Luther/King visited me at my house the next day to report on his meeting with the Terran Secretary of the Anorexic Party at her office in Hong Kong. Upon delivering our official response, Dr. King was kept waiting in her outer office for almost two hours, during which he reported hearing muffled shouting and "what sounded to me like three gun shots in rapid succession."

A few minutes later, the Party Secretary sent out her personal assistant with a sealed communiqué to me.

We opened it together.

Manchu Ellins was not going to be the candidate of the Anorexic Party after all. My response had evidently caused the Anorexic leadership to retool their own plans and we were going to be facing a campaign of an entirely different sort.

The official candidate of the Anorexic Party for the governorship of earth was the Reverend Doctor Sun Amen Chill, Pastor of the Newer Light Televangelical Cathedral in Lakewood, California—and the election had been scheduled for October 31ˢᵗ—just seven weeks away.

The date of the election, Martin Luther pointed out to me, was not significant only because it was eve of the Christian holiday honoring the dearly departed. It was also the anniversary of that day in 1517 when Luther had launched the Christian Reformation by posting his ninety-five theses to the Castle Church in Wittenberg, Germany. Lucifer, not the greatest mathematician in the universes, evidently liked whole numbers; the Interregnum would begin and end on the same date.

"What does this change of candidates mean?" I asked Dr. King.

"It means," he said, "that the Anorexic Party has an open line between its offices in Heaven and earth … and that Satan is very, *very* upset."

"That's a good thing, isn't it?" I asked.

Martin Luther King paused a long moment. "It means that you've caught her off guard, which is good. But don't take this as a sign that we can let our guard down. History often shows that when Satan gets upset, bad things happen to good people."

Over the next month, things on earth continued to be very quiet.

Say it with me: too quiet.

As I pointed out right at the beginning of this narrative, radio talk show hosts have to keep up with the news, especially if anything controversial or dramatic has happened. Usually that's what people want to talk about. I was in the habit of scanning through three daily newspapers, watching the morning news shows, and listening to what other radio hosts were talking about.

But the newspapers were running back-section features on the front page and talk show hosts were focusing on sports, fashion, their mother's favorite recipes, and entertainment gossip.

Golda Meir had warned us to be prepared for disasters. Not only wasn't there a single natural disaster or new terrorist attack being reported anywhere, even long-standing political feuds started relaxing.

Forest fires were down. It was raining where it was too dry and sunny where the ground was already too soggy. The weather was good and the temperatures mild.

New peace initiatives were being proffered by both sides in traditional global hot spots.

Nobody was rioting anywhere, or even protesting.

There were no labor strikes or lockouts.

The latest unemployment figures were down and consumer spending was up. The stock market was on an upswing again.

Banks started lowering their interest rates for consumer loans, and raising the interest rates they were paying on savings and money-market accounts.

Congress had just passed a repeal of the capital gains tax and the inheritance tax, and the president announced that federal drug-war funds earmarked for the Drug Enforcement Agency were being reassigned to the Centers for Disease Control and Prevention.

China announced that it was abolishing the death penalty for political crimes, and offering a general amnesty to most dissidents.

The Los Angeles Chief of Police held a press conference claiming that his just-implemented "Officer Friendly" program was working immediately; emergency operators were reporting that violent crime calls were down eighty-five percent in the last month. But so were 911 calls on domestic disputes, and I didn't see how having jollier police officers in patrol cars could affect that very much.

The Anorexic Party had yet to avail themselves of an opportunity to make a campaign presentation in any astral plane. Nor was there any indication in media available to the mortal population that they were about to be polled on any important decision.

There was an off-year-election coming up early November in the U.S., but the most controversial voter initiatives in California were suddenly thrown off the ballot by the California Supreme Court, and even their sponsors didn't seem too upset about it.

Burr's spooks in the astral plane reported to him that the frequency of human nightmares was also down significantly. Perhaps that explained why incidents of road rage, and traffic accidents, were down as well.

People were sleeping better.

The religious revival that Mencken had warned us would appear following worldwide disasters had also not manifested.

I tuned in to Sun Amen Chill's Sunday morning sermon and instead of his usual rap about the salvation that awaited us if we were washed in the blood of Jesus (is that what Jesus was burning in his pipe?), he preached from his pulpit that this was a wonderful day for everyone to go with their family and friends on a picnic or to a ball game.

Lucifer's operatives on earth had been pulled off all their usual jobs and it looked as if their new product was sweetness and light.

I had a bad feeling about this.

Chapter Seventeen

On Saturday, October 8th, I received a report that a tunnel had opened up briefly above Lakewood, California, and a lone occupant had flown out. Our militia had given chase but whoever it was had managed to elude them.

In King Solomon's legal opinion this was a clear treaty violation, and Dr. King filed a formal protest with the Anorexic Party on our behalf. The Anorexic Party's official response was uncharacteristic: they admitted the breach and asked us what balancing we wished in compensation.

We answered that we were going to hold them to an equivalent protocol exception of our choosing to be redeemed at any point before or after the election. Amazingly, they agreed.

They were being way too affable. Now I was really worried.

A bell went off in my head announcing that I had an instant message on my internal desktop. It was steganographically coded for maximum privacy, and I had pretty good confidence that not only couldn't it be intercepted or decoded, but that it wouldn't even be recognized as a message. The message's private key signature proved that it was from Lindbergh. When decoded, the message in its entirety was, "Success. Awaiting your signal."

I found out what I had to be worried about the next morning at 8:00 AM local time, on the Reverend Doctor Sun Amen Chill's top-rated Sunday broadcast program, a one-hour globally telecast worship service named *Morning Glory*.

Sun Amen Chill wasn't your typical TV evangelist.

He was built like a football player, was as good-looking as a movie star, had a singing voice reminiscent of Jim Morrison, and always began his program by running out to his pulpit like a game-show host, with brassy theme music appropriate for a late-night talk show. He was always dressed in a designer suit of the latest fashion.

His denomination was nominally Baptist, but he was famous for dispensing with dogma and inviting Catholics, Jews, Muslims, Buddhists, Native American Indians, and even Wiccans to join him on his pulpit and offer up whatever prayers to the Deity they wished to, in the language of their own traditions.

His sermons preached directly from the Bible, but he always managed to relate biblical passages to whatever was in the news, and his sermons often had the flavor more of a stand-up TV comic doing "blend" than of a traditional religious service.

His musical choices were even more unusual. Instead of the standard program of praise and worship music, he managed each week to astonish his TV viewers with musical talent worthy of *Saturday Night Live* or the *Tonight Show*. Musical guests on his program had included Grammy-winning artists in rock music, classical, jazz, and country. He'd performed more duets with other singers than Sammy Davis, Jr.

And it probably won't surprise you that Caulinn Helms' grunge band, Seminal Lunch, had appeared on the program over half-a-dozen times, four-letter words and all, but bringing their loyal followers into the fold with them.

Reverend Chill let his band do an opening number while he ran through the front rows of his congregation, kissing women and shaking men's hands. Then it was his custom to run back to his pulpit, grab a mike and join his band in an opening song of his own composition, usually something reminiscent of David Bowie or Sting.

This was always followed by the words, "Please stand. Let us pray."

But something was different this Sunday.

When he returned to his pulpit he waved his bandleader into silence, said, "Please be seated," and waited for silence.

His congregation, many more of them kids and teenagers than you might expect, looked surprised but expectant. They knew he was a showman—that's what brought them here—but he was breaking format.

"Brothers and sisters," he began, "there are moments in history that come without warning and change everything forever. Some of these moments are terrible, and we say they are a 'catastrophe.' We have had way too many of these: earthquakes, sneak attacks that begin great wars, assassinations.

"But there are also transforming moments that are wonderful and great ... and there's a word for that, too: *eucatastrophe*. The greatest of these moments, until now, was when our Lord Jesus Christ rose from the dead, and showed us the path to Heaven.

"I have been blessed with an honor that I have done nothing to deserve, but that as an obedient servant I can only thank God for permitting me. There has been a new incarnation, one which proves to us the reality of the Bible, of God, and of Heaven. We have always thought that the New Age would begin with the return of Jesus to cast Satan out of his throne on earth, but I have come to learn that this is only one of the prophecies of Saint John the Divine that were in error.

"My brothers and sisters, it is the very mother of the human race that has come back to us directly from her home in Heaven, the great spirit who is known as the wife of our Lord and Savior, and who was here at the very beginning of our creation.

"Tonight, everyone on earth will have a dream, in which she will visit you personally and confirm to you the truth of my words.

"Brothers and sisters, what you are about to see is not stage magic, it is not trick photography, it is not a special effect, computer generated or otherwise. The members of my congregation who are here and watching this pulpit will be able to give you personal eye-witness testimony to what they see at this service.

"They will be able to confirm from the evidence of their own eyes the reality of the miracle you who cannot be here in person with us are about to see. We will invite the news media to join us after this service to observe and see for themselves whether or not these are genuine miracles. We invite any scientist or other skeptic who wishes to do so to set up experiments verifying this reality.

"But right now—live, in resurrected flesh, and making her first open appearance on earth since the days of Eden when she was our mother, I give you—*Eve!*"

The band began playing ethereal chords, a musical stairway, broken by the herald of trumpets … then, looking absolutely virginal and gorgeous, dressed in a white satin gown, long red hair flowing behind her, Lucifer flew out from the wings, directly over the congregation slow enough for them to touch her hands, which she extended down to them, and as they gasped in astonishment, she flew back to the pulpit and landed next to the Reverend Doctor Sun Amen Chill.

Suddenly spotlights backlit her in a glorious corona, as she smiled benevolently, and her first words rang out to everyone watching with a voice like butter:

"My children, I have come home."

I looked over to my right and saw that my chief of staff, Robert Heinlein, had materialized and was standing next to me, watching my TV.

"Oh, boy," I said to him. "Am I ever in big trouble."

Chapter Eighteen

Within minutes after Eve's premiere appearance on *Morning Glory*, all hell broke loose.

Television crews, print reporters, scientists from Cal Tech, skeptics including a stage magician who was famous for debunking psychic phenomena, politicians, Hollywood celebrities, and just about anyone else who could get onto the freeways into Lakewood descended onto the vast manicured lawn surrounding Reverend Chill's Newer Light Cathedral.

Lucifer performed just about every miracle in the Bible. There was a duck pond on the church grounds. Lucifer parted the water, walked on the water, and turned the water into wine. She waved her hand and suddenly the pond was full of fishes. One of the ducks had passed away and she raised it from the dead.

Manchu Ellins rang my doorbell and personally served me with a communiqué from Anorexic Party headquarters. There was a substitution on their ballot line.

Sun Amen Chill was off their ballot line.

Eve was on.

I called an immediate emergency session of the central committee, and Heinlein and I flew back to Mount Shasta. There was a substitution in my council since Lindbergh/Lewis/Polo was off on assignment. Taking his place at the round table was Sir Isaac Newton.

Jefferson and Franklin's legal analysis of Lucifer's

sudden entry into the race provided us with little le-
verage. She had made no untruthful statements herself, nor even lent the appearance of truth to a false
statement, since everything the Reverend Chill had
said was carefully worded to stay within the bounds
of semantic accuracy. The Anorexic Party had made
no statement that we could object to, no grounds for
us to demand a retraction.

Lucifer had performed no miracles above π on the
Aquinas Scale.

She had not misrepresented to the people of earth
her identity or her role in human history.

And there was nothing in the treaty that prevented
the substitution of a name on a ballot line at any time
previous to the opening of the campaign with its first
dream presentation.

The only treaty violation the Anorexic Party had
committed was her opening a tunnel to come to earth.
Other than that, they had played strictly by the rules.

We'd been sucker punched.

"My friends," I told them. "I'm not going to make
any excuses. This disaster is directly due to my arro-
gance and ineptness. If we lose this war, there is nobody to blame but me."

"Sir, with all due respect," said General Patton,
"that's hogwash. Never apologize to your men. You
lead them, they follow, that's all. I apologized to one
of my men once and I regret it to this day. You made a
command decision, one—may I add—that looked good
to all of us. Victory is never assured. All we can give it
is the best we have within us."

"Hear, hear," said voices all around the table.

"I believe General Patton has expressed all of our feelings in this matter," said Jefferson. "We still have complete confidence in you."

I felt like crying but held myself in check. This was no time to come across as the weakest link.

"Ladies and Gentlemen, I thank you for your vote of confidence in me. Now let's get back to work. Is there anyone at this table who thinks the strategy I outlined at our last session, of allowing Lucifer to run unopposed, has a chance in hell of succeeding?"

The silence was deafening.

"I concur. Mr. Attorney General, since the Anorexic Party has now made two substitutions on their ballot line, am I correct in concluding that we have the right to do so as well?"

"That is true," Jefferson told me, "but only if we act immediately. Lucifer's dream presentation starts as early as seven hours from now, triggering the active campaign. Any substitutions on the ballot must be served on the Anorexics before then."

"Okay, then we haven't time to shilly-shally," I said. "It's my opinion that the only candidate who would be able to take on Lucifer after the show she's put on today would be one of the Trinity."

"But that's expressly forbidden by the terms of the treaty," said Benjamin Franklin.

"We've got one treaty violation to our benefit coming to us," I said. "I asked for a blank check in payment when they violated the treaty, and they signed it. I say, at this point, we are entitled to put one of the Trinity on the ballot."

"That may be true from a legalistic standpoint," said

Aaron Burr, "but it still leaves us without an active candidate to campaign here on earth. If we put one of the Trinity on the ballot, they will still be legally restricted from opening a tunnel to come here."

"I disagree," said King Solomon. "Placing a different name on the ballot isn't anything they need to grant us as a special favor; we're entitled to do that anyway, just so long as it's done by tonight. The treaty exception due us may include nullifying that clause which forbids the Trinity from standing for office. It's my legal opinion that in compensation for Lucifer violating the terms of the treaty by coming to earth after Satan 001, we are entitled to bring in one of the Trinity here."

"Keep in mind," said Patton, "if we are seen trying to open up a tunnel, you're going to see Satan's military forces stationed on earth launching a counterattack immediately. They're not going to care about the legalisms of a treaty at that point. With everything at stake, they'll fight."

"General, can you secure this facility we're in right now to withstand such an attack?"

"It was constructed for that very purpose, sir," Patton said. "We're inside a fortress."

"So we open up the tunnel in here."

"With what?" W.C. Fields asked. "Do you have a church key?"

"I'm not going to discuss that until the time is right," I said. "Our first order of business is to decide which of the Trinity we need to run."

"If we run God or Jesus, Lucifer will turn this into a sex war," said Ayn Rand. "I have never been in favor of running a woman for a man's job, but logic dictates the way to put the lie to Eve's claim that she is the mother of the human race is to show the people of earth its real mother, Maryse."

"My dear," said C.S. Lewis, "I tremble at the very thought of disagreeing with you, but I must. Our celestial mother, Maryse, does not have what political analysts call 'name recognition.'"

"The Virgin Mary isn't good enough name recognition for you?" replied Rand. "Lucifer is using her earthborn name, why can't Maryse?"

"'The Virgin Mary' on our ballot line would deliver a billion Roman Catholic votes," said Mark Twain.

"But you would lose a billion Islamic votes," replied Sa'di of Shiraz. "I'm sorry but Muslims simply won't vote for a woman to rule them on either ballot line. The world of Islam would simply boycott the ballot."

"You're forgetting Muslim women," Rand said.

"There is no League of Women Voters in the world of Islam," answered Sa'di. "Our women are accustomed to doing what their fathers and husbands tell them to do."

The silence that followed showed that Sa'di had made his point.

"Then we are deciding between the Father and the Son," I said. "More comments?"

"God has better name recognition worldwide," said H.L. Mencken, "but nobody on earth knows what he looks like and—with no disrespect to you, sir—his appearing similar to a radio-talk-show host might be fatally distracting to the voters. Nor do I think his appearing as a Burning Bush will prevail in an election against a beautiful woman, no matter what he says or what miracles he performs."

"Then we are running a husband against his ex-wife?" I asked.

"That will be our Savior's problem, sir," said Dr. King, "not ours."

"It's my decision unless God fires me from my appointment as campaign manager of the Party of God," I said.

"If Jesus is the candidate," said Golda Meir, "you're going to lose the Jewish vote."

"What is that?" said Sa'di. "Ten or twelve million votes out of seven billion?"

"That could be five times your margin of victory in a tight race," said Meir. "Look at Florida in the 2000 U.S. presidential election."

"Jesus is one of Islam's prophets," said Sa'di. "I believe I can deliver at least a billion Muslim votes for Jesus, just so long as we distance him from Christian history and Christian doctrine. In what sort of election can you throw away that?"

"What about Hindus, Buddhists, and Chinese atheists?" asked Shaw. "Who has the best chance at their votes?"

"I don't see that Lucifer has any better chance of locking up those votes on name recognition alone than we do," said Rand, "no matter which of the Trinity we run."

"Any other comments?" I asked.

There was silence.

Mencken turned to Golda Meir and said, "Suppose we put Jesus on the ballot as Adam. Would that play with Jewish voters?"

"It couldn't hurt," she said. "We might even do better if our Hebrew campaign handouts referred to him as Rabbi Yeshovuah."

"The name 'Adam' would probably do better than 'Jesus' with secular voters and perhaps even pagans," said Mencken. "I could set up a focus group—"

"We don't have time for a focus group," cut in Jefferson. "Our ballot deadline is in just a few hours."

There was a silence, which I took as my opportunity to take back control of the meeting.

"I was born Jewish," I said. "You all know my relationship to God, how I'd do anything for him. But God gave me the job of winning this election, and I think Mr. Mencken is right. God hasn't spent as much time walking precincts as Jesus has, and in my opinion that dirty-feet human experience is what's needed in this election."

I took a deep breath.

I continued, "I also think there's no point playing games with the ballot, trying to conceal the full identity of our candidate. He is who he is, take him or leave him."

Here I go again, I thought.

I said, "It's my decision that the candidate of the Party of God for the governorship of earth in the October 31st election is our Lord and Savior, Jesus the Christ, also known as Adam. Dr. King, please notify the Anorexic Party of our ballot-line substitution at the conclusion of this session."

"Yes, sir," said Martin Luther/King.

"Menu," I said.

My desktop appeared before my eyes and I double

clicked on an icon.

"General Lindbergh, can you hear me?"

"Yes, sir."

"Please open Tunnel Gates P2 and E1, using my desktop's current position as terminal locus."

A tunnel irised open behind me, the bottom level with the floor.

I stood, and as I stood, so did everyone else.

Charles Lindbergh, who had formerly been Meriwether Lewis, who before that had been Marco Polo, stepped into the room and saluted me.

I returned his salute.

He moved to a position standing near the table.

A moment later, everyone in the room bowed their heads as Jesus stepped into the room.

Jesus turned to me. "Well done, my good and faithful servant," he said, and kissed me on both cheeks.

Some days it pays to get out of bed.

Chapter Nineteen

There was one immediate surprise waiting for me. It happened when Jesus walked around the table, greeting everyone.

When Jesus reached Robert A. Heinlein, he hugged him and said, "Judas, how are you, my old friend?"

I nearly fainted.

I turned to Heinlein. "You were Judas in a previous life? *The* Judas? Thirty-pieces-of silver Judas?"

Robert Heinlein and Jesus both looked at the expression on my face, then looked at each other, and burst out laughing.

"Tell me, Duj," said Jesus. "How long do you think one of my apostles could hide an evil plot to betray me, given my power to look directly into men's souls?"

I smiled sheepishly. "I keep forgetting to place the historical facts into the context of my new knowledge," I said.

"Wisdom takes time," said Jesus. "At the last Passover seder, when I said 'He who dips after me will betray me,' it wasn't a prophecy. Why would anyone who was really secretly plotting to betray me reveal himself by dipping after I said that? It's ridiculous. No. I was asking for a volunteer for the nastiest, dirtiest job I'd ever given any of my disciples. To betray me, take money for it to keep my real purpose a secret, and watch me die on a cross in horrible pain. Then, to make it even worse, he'd have to put up with his name being spit upon for two millennia, by people calling themselves Christians who can't read a simple paragraph with proper comprehension. I granted him special dispensation to hang himself so he could be the first of my apostles to be resurrected."

Jesus put his arm around Judas's shoulders. He looked like he was trying to hold back tears.

"It was so terrible a mission," Jesus continued, "that I didn't feel I could just order one of my apostles to do it. This merchant marine turned commercial broker, at that moment in time, before any of the other apostles had started their missions and found their own courage, had more sheer guts than the other apostles all put together. He just took a sprig of bitter herb, dipped it into the salt water after me, and said, "Master, you've got yourself a boy."

Jesus turned to the others in the room. "No matter what else happens in the next three weeks," he said, "I will take it as a personal favor if all of you do your best to set the record straight about my most loyal disciple, Judas."

And at that celestially perfect moment, Judas Iscariot, under his original name, got his first standing ovation in history.

Things went into high gear after that. The election was only three weeks away and with her slickly produced dream campaign spot that night, Lucifer immediately established herself as the frontrunner. I wondered which Hollywood director Lucifer had working her media when I realized that it was a pointless question—she could have her pick of the best of them, and they were probably donating their services for free.

Meanwhile, we were playing catch-up.

Jesus had visited earth only a couple of times since his crucifixion, and hadn't been allowed to set foot on earth at all in almost five centuries. So he decided to rely on the political judgments of his more up-to-date earthborn campaign staff. He reconfirmed my job as his campaign manager, as well as all my duty assignments, and when we all took our seats at the round table again, I continued to chair the Central Committee while Jesus just listened unless one of us asked his opinion directly.

We didn't know precisely what our order of play was yet—a lot of campaigning is taking advantage of opportunities as they come up—but we knew that before Lucifer could get too much momentum we had to introduce Jesus to the world again.

Ironically, Lucifer had done half my job for me already. The publicity coup she and Reverend Chill had pulled off had the whole world talking about God, Adam and Eve, and the life of Jesus again. Our problem wasn't so much going to be convincing the world that Jesus was real—Lucifer had already solved that problem for us — as it was getting out a more accurate version of historical events and getting the news coverage spinning our way.

Speaking in general about the next three weeks of campaigning, I have to acknowledge that both Jesus and I were relying on the judgments of men and women who'd had vastly more hands-on political experience that we'd had.

Most campaign decisions I immediately shoved onto the lap of my chief of staff, now holding the title of Deputy Campaign Director. Robert Heinlein had been heavily involved in political campaigning back in the 1930's, even running for office himself, and one of his forty-plus books was a manual on electoral campaigning titled *Take Back Your Government.*

Heinlein, in turn, was making maximum use of our central committee's top political operatives, people like Thomas Jefferson, Aaron Burr, Golda Meir, and Benjamin Franklin/H.L. Mencken. Among them they had enough campaign experience that they could have elected a Republican as mayor of Chicago.

Mencken/Franklin stayed in his job as the campaign's press secretary, but now he was going to have to manage daily contact with the mortal world's news media.

It was clear this was no longer going to be a campaign restricted to dreamland, although that was still an important part of our media creation. Much of our campaign was now going to be in the waking world of mortal men, and Jesus was going to have to be as in-your-face as any other office seeker.

Right after he'd served the Anorexic Party with our just-under-the-deadline notice of ballot-line substitution, I gave Dr. Martin Luther King, Jr., the job of being Jesus' advance man for rallies, demonstrations, and personal appearances. Martin Luther King knew as much about preparing a crowd and stirring them up as anyone in human history, including the Lord, himself.

Mark Twain and Bernard Shaw teamed up as Jesus'

main speechwriters—although Thomas Jefferson and Franklin/Mencken were also submitting speeches — but I was giving Dr. King everybody's final drafts before Jesus used them and Martin was spicing up their rhetorical flourishes.

I gave W.C. Fields a job that is crucial to every successful campaign, but which few campaigns even admit exists. He was our joke writer. It was his job to stay close to Jesus at all times and on a moment's notice be prepared to feed him snappy one-liners.

Not that Jesus wasn't a master at snappy come-backs on his own anyway.

The central committee debated hard (but not long; we didn't have the time) about what the theme of the campaign should be. We discussed using "The Second Coming." But we decided the word "coming" has too much of a sexual connotation for use to a G-rated audience and when you're in advertising, you never want to use a slogan your competitors can turn back on you. We played around with all the variations we could think of—"He's Back" or "The Homecoming" — but they all sounded like slogans for a movie sequel.

We examined traditional themes associated with Jesus—even considered basing the campaign on Christmas and Santa Clause—but it just came across as stale and hokey. "Fisher of Men" just wasn't going to work, either; the unavoidable imagery of having a fishhook down your throat was just too icky.

Finally, we decided to modify the idea of "savior" just slightly, and base our campaign imagery on rescue workers already associated with saving people when they were in trouble.

We didn't have any trouble at all finding firefighters, paramedics, or ER doctors and triage nurses who wanted to pose with Jesus. As you can imagine, a lot of them had prayed to Jesus for courage in dire moments, and this was the sort of prayer Jesus had been permitted by treaty to answer.

That's how our campaign theme became, "Your 911 call's been answered. Jesus is here to rescue you."

We decided it would be in poor taste to pose Jesus wearing any sort of uniform. That's why, in our campaign handouts, posters, billboards, TV spots, and dreamscapes, we showed Jesus in his traditional robes, working side-by-side with firefighters, EMT's, and ER personnel.

We needed to make a decision about which image of Jesus to use during the campaign: the short, bearded, Middle-Eastern Jew who had been born to Joseph and Mary, or the taller, blond, clean-shaven, more-movie-star-like Adam.

That was a no-brainer.

But our first job was to find the right venue to launch our campaign and introduce our candidate to the voters. Lucifer had set the bar very high for show-biz value but for once I wanted the good guys to outdo her.

We called in some outside talent of our own, and I think you'll agree that what we came up with for Jesus first reappearance on earth on Tuesday, October 11th, was quite spectacular.

Chapter Twenty

Until Zero Hour on October 11th, Jesus' return to earth was the closest held military secret since D-Day.

The Anorexic Party had to be notified that we were placing Jesus' name on the ballot, but they had no way of knowing that we wouldn't be running an absentee campaign for him. As far as they knew, since they had thrown up what they considered an impenetrable blockade around the Celestial Palace, we had no way of getting any of the Trinity out of their "St. Helena" exile, much less squire one of them back to earth.

I'm not going to take even a smidgeon of credit for the plan by which we opened up the tunnel from the Celestial Palace to our fortress on Mt. Shasta and returned Jesus to earth. The idea, the plan, and the entire solo operation was entirely General Lindbergh's.

Charles Lindbergh had more flying hours than anyone else in human history and he had established speed records that even today are classified military secrets. His proposal to me, made privately just after my first meeting with the Central Committee, was to place himself on round-the-clock watch for the possibility that the Anorexics would break treaty and open up a tunnel. If and when they did, he was going to fly like all get-out and place himself inside that tunnel before it closed up again.

Once inside, he was going to climb into the auto-control systems and program them to open gates at his command. He then opened up a communications gate back to my desktop so tiny that it was undetectable. He'd found a similar microgate already in operation between Heaven and the Anorexic Party headquarters in Hong Kong, but left it alone because tampering with it would have alerted the enemy to his presence.

He used the new microgate he'd set up to send me the first coded message. Then Lindy hunkered down, took some sandwiches and a thermos of coffee out of a satchel he'd packed, and waited for my signal.

You know, things just go so well when you can work with the best of the best.

For once Duj Pepperman, Los Angeles's top-rated evening-drive-time radio-talk-show host, was going to be useful to the campaign.

I didn't base the appeal of my current show on guests so much as call-ins. But I'd been in the radio business for most of my adult life, and over thirty years, with changing tastes and formats, I'd had more top-rated celebrities sitting at my microphone than you can find in the audience of most award shows.

Radio is a volatile business. I'd always prepared for a day when my ARB's might take an unexpected dip and station management might decide a restructuring of my format might be needed. Celebrity guests could be good for ratings in a crunch.

I'd sent out expensive gift boxes of Mrs. Fields cookies every Christmas to my "A list," and with the thank-you letters I got, I'd kept my Rolodex up to date.

I needed to get an immediate booking with the top-rated syndicated TV talk-show host in the country—the man who knocked Oprah into the number two ratings slot the way she'd once pounced on Phil Donahue—and when you're in a hurry, you can't call a show's booker; you have to have the unlisted phone number of the star, himself.

I had the unlisted, NSA-safe spread-spectrum, voice-encrypted, PCS cell phone number of Uncle Nimlash.

I caught him early Monday morning, October 10th, as he was driving his classic Tucker '48 into the parking lot of CBS's Television City. He had a policy of answering his phone by yelling, "Yeah?!" at the top of his lungs to intimidate anyone he didn't want to talk to; I'd gotten used to it and didn't let it bother me.

"Hey, don't shout at me, you filthy bastard," I answered him, "or I'll stuff a banana up the tailpipe of that old junker of yours."

"Hey, Pepperman, you old fart, how're they hangin?"

"More snugly than you'd believe, my friend," I told him.

"Hold on a second while I unhook my phone," he said, and after a few seconds I heard a door slam, the chirping of an alarm, and he came back on, "I'm walking into my office," he told me, "You have thirty seconds to sell me on whatever favor you want."

"It's not what you can do for me, Neil," I said, "it's what I can do for you."

"Bullshit walks," he said. "Give me the deal, not a blow job."

"One question first," I asked him. "Have you booked Eve?"

"Yeah, right," he said. "I told my bookers I'd give the one who got me Eve a year's salary as bonus, and they came up with bupkas. She's not doing any show where she needs to answer questions. Why, are you saying you can deliver her for a sitdown? Name your price if you can."

"Forget Eve; she's yesterday's news. I can give you Jesus Christ."

Under normal circumstances, Nimlash would have made a wisecrack and hung up on me ... but Eve's appearance yesterday had shaken the foundations of "normal."

Cal Tech hadn't released its formal report yet but inside sources were leaking a draft that said in its executive summary, "After presenting this personage with an extensive series of controlled tests in our own laboratories under conditions we controlled exclusively and which she could not possibly have anticipated or manipulated, we have found no evidence of fraud and must allow for the possibility that a genuine series of paranormal actions have indeed been performed."

"How much?" he said.

"Not a penny to us, but there are conditions. It's tomorrow or never. We get the whole hour. Jesus will be bringing a slew of guests; you don't see the list. No breaks, commercial, promo, or PSA's, except for FCC mandated station ID's. We do the show live in your New York time slot, all satellite uplinks running, plus you put your watermark on it and allow every other network, independent station, and cable outlet who wants it to carry it live or delayed. All newscasts and magazines get to use the footage until November 1ˢᵗ. We'll provide our own security detail. I'll be faxing over some sheet music; you keep your band on over-time after today's taping, rehearsing it with stand-ins for the vocal parts, who'll be singing nonsense lyrics that match the real ones. If a word of who your guest is gets out to anyone prior to five minutes before air time tomorrow, including to your producer, your wife, or your make-up artist, we'll know it immediately and walk. But you get your syndicate to promote this like the Second Coming, because, my friend, that's exactly what I'm offering you. Do we have a deal?"

He sounded like he was breathing heavily. I extended my presence to make sure he wasn't having a heart attack. His blood pressure was 160 over 90 but his heartbeat was steady.

"Duj, you got me a job interview when I was stuck in Tucson doing weather. You know how little weather there is to report on in Tucson? I've never forgotten that. But I have to ask you. Is this one-hundred per-cent? Because this means I have to call in every marker I've got and tell my affiliates I'm ending the show if they don't carry me live tomorrow."

"It's one-hundred-percent, 24 karat guaranteed," I said.

"Then, he said, "deal. But if I don't have a faxed contract from you in my office within 20 minutes, then no deal. I'm sending a notary over to your condo in one hour to witness your signature."

"The Fedexed contract with my notarized signature was signed for by your secretary eight minutes ago," I said, "and your word was all I needed to proceed."

He paused.

"You're ending my career if one of us is being scammed, Duj, and I don't think either of our business managers will be able to save even our pension annuities from the lawsuits. Matter of fact, we'd both be lucky to stay out of prison."

He hung up.

Part 3
Oprah, Eat Your Heart Out

Chapter Twenty-One

Uncle Nimlash bought promos on a variety of broadcast and cable networks from prime time to late night that very Monday:

"An extra special *Uncle Nimlash Show,* live, with a *surprise* special guest. Tune in tomorrow to find out all about Eve! Is she who she claims to be or is she the ultimate scam artist? Tomorrow, on *Uncle Nimlash.*"

The promos continued Tuesday on the network's morning shows, so that within two hours of the live broadcast—3:00 PM in New York, 12:00 noon in L.A.— Uncle Nimlash had received word that 93% of the local stations that carried his show, including all his major-city network affiliates who were postponing highly-rated network-feed soap operas, were carrying his live broadcast.

We in the campaign worried that the Anorexic Party might figure out that it was Jesus who was going to be appearing on the show and launch an all-out attack to stop it—anything from firing a cruise missile into Television City to knocking out the power grid feeding Los Angeles—but our agents never detected any activity.

We were praying—we were counting on—Lucifer's intelligence analysts concluding either that Uncle Nimlash's surprise guest was going to be a psychic-debunker, or at worst some resurrected historical figure who was going to "come out" to the mortal world in an attempt to play down Eve's celestial importance.

Patton took personal charge of setting up security perimeters for the show, utilizing the talents of resurrected Secret Service agents who were part of our militia. We actually had Jesus and all our other guests sequestered in a locked-off vacant studio within Television City by 4:00 AM, and from that moment on, Zero minus eight hours, we had our own people in charge of all access and communication at Television City, and a security team performing all the cautionary functions you'd expect from a visit to a television studio by a head of state.

The rehearsal of the musical number we planned was finessed by having Uncle Nimlash's band play in his studio, and the music piped in to the studio we were using as our temporary headquarters. Even at this late hour, for extra security, we had our chorus rehearsing using nonsense lyrics:

> Hand me some more cola!
> Hand me some more steak!
> Bring me some fried chicken!
> Lend a piece of cake!

We relied on our own make-up artists and wardrobe crew so no one from Uncle Nimlash's production company would have any contact with us until just before air time.

We brought in our own team of stand-ins to Uncle Nimlash's studio for the technical rehearsal, but even they didn't know for whom they were standing in. We had warned Uncle Nimlash to make sure his camera operators and booth technicians for this show had experience covering live news and sporting events;

most of what we were about to do was going to have to be caught on shoulder-mounted cameras with quick lens adjustments.

At Zero minus sixty minutes, I met Uncle Nimlash in his studio to hand his director a DVD-R disk which had pre-generated graphic titles and archived film and video footage, for each of our extra guests. One of our security agents shadowed the director from that moment on to make sure the information on that disk wasn't leaked outside the studio prematurely.

We allowed Uncle Nimlash to file in their studio audience at Zero minus thirty minutes, and we had a squad of our people walk through the seats peeping everyone's soul to make sure no operatives from the Anorexic party had slipped by our outer checkpoints.

At Zero minus fifteen minutes we brought our people out of sequester and positioned them behind the curtain of Uncle Nimlash's studio.

We felt confident enough that our secret had been kept that we ended our news embargo five minutes early. We handed out the full list of names, including Jesus, to Uncle Nimlash's staff, and allowed them to transmit a prerecorded flash not only to all their affiliates but also to all the network headquarters, telling them what hard news they were about to break.

This was the first moment that Uncle Nimlash looked as if he *wasn't* about to have a stroke. With the network news departments, themselves, cutting into their daytime broadcast with breaking news, his network affiliates who had earlier committed to him weren't going to be blamed by either their networks or the soap fans for ignoring their scheduled programming.

"One minute," said the director, over the studio loud-speakers.

The stage lights came up to full power and the band stopped tuning and brought their instruments up, waiting for the drummer's stick beats.

I was standing backstage next to Jesus and I noticed he looked nervous. "After being nailed to a cross, *this* frightens you?" I asked him.

Jesus smiled weakly. "I've never sung before an audience before," he said.

Oh, God, I thought, silently enough, I hoped, that Jesus wouldn't pick up on my thought: What if the Son of God was tone deaf? I hadn't had the guts to ask him to rehearse.

I had no more time to worry.

The director was counting down, "eight ... seven ... six ... five ... four ..." then counted the last three numbers with his fingers, silently, and cued the bandleader.

The bandleader clicked his drumsticks together four times, and the Nimlashers launched into their brassy theme song.

Up in the booth, behind glass, I could see Uncle Nimlash's announcer, Cineman Hulls, holding the script we'd written for him. No one aside from Neil Nimlash, himself, had seen it prior to the broadcast.

Hulls got his cue through earphones.

"Live, from Television City in Hollywood, it's your Uncle Nimlash Show! Today we have the most spectacular line up of musical talent ever assembled on the same stage, to be led in a new song composed specially for this broadcast! Ladies and Gentlemen, may I present to you, back from the grave, here's Jerry Garcia!"

Garcia flew out into the audience the way Lucifer had (okay, we stole the bit; it was a good visual), then landed on stage.

The audience went wild.

Cineman Hulls read off each name, with one more of our resurrected celebrities flying into the studio to join Jerry Garcia.

"John Lennon!

"Billie Holiday!

"Frank Sinatra!

"Maurice Chevalier!

"Patsy Cline!

"Jimi Hendrix!

"Enrico Caruso!

"Ethel Merman!

"Roy Orbison!

"Marvin Gaye!

"Dean Martin!

"Buddy Holly!

"Judy Garland!

"Burl Ives!

"Edith Piaf!

"John Denver!

"Lily Pons!

"Nat King Cole!

"Laverne and Maxene Andrews!

"Bing Crosby!

"Hank Williams!

"Sammy Davis, Jr.!

"Dorothy Dandridge!

"Frank Zappa!

"Mel Tormé!

"Janis Joplin!

"Mama Cass Elliot!

"Jim Morrison!

"Perry Como!

"...and Elvis Presley!

"Ladies and gentlemen, I give to you, *the New Grateful Dead*!"

They all joined hands and started swaying back and forth, as the band began playing the opening chords of the special song that Lennon and Garcia had composed for this occasion:

> When you're low and luckless
> When troubles never cease
> Ask him for a helping hand
> He will bring you peace!

"Ladies and gentlemen," announced Cineman Hulls, reverently, "the next voice you hear will be God's firstborn son and the firstborn man, he who brought back to life all the wonderful people you see here before you. You know him as Adam, the first man, and you know him as the savior of all humanity, I give you, *Jesus Christ*!"

A clear Irish tenor voice, reminiscent of Dennis Day, rang out mellifluously into the studio:

> I only want to give you
> The greatest gift of all
> When dreams look past tomorrow
> You can hear my call!

And Jesus walked—not flew, but walked—onto the

stage, dressed in his traditional robes, holding a handheld mike.

The New Grateful Dead behind him sang in chorus:

> Hands across the water
> Hands across the land
> Bring the little children
> Lend a helping hand!

Jesus soloed:

> Your creed is unimportant
> Nor color of your face
> I'm here to be redeemer
> Of the human race!

The chorus:

> Hands Across the water
> Hands Across the sky
> Paradise is waiting
> You don't have to die!

And Jesus reprised the first verse:

> When you're low and luckless
> When troubles never cease
> Ask me for a helping hand
> I will bring you peace!

And Jesus and the chorus sang the final chorus together:

> Hands across the water
> Hands across the world
> I am here to save you
> Every boy and girl!

The audience went crazy.

The interview program that Uncle Nimlash did for the rest of his hour with Jesus and the assembled performers was almost anticlimactic after the opening song, but it was a way of presenting our campaign platform for the first time.

Jesus was careful to say nothing negative about Eve, perhaps disappointing that segment of the viewing audience who had tuned in expecting debunking or scandal. He did not "out" her alternate identities as Lucifer, Lilith, or Satan, and stuck to promoting his own positive message of love and the universal brotherhood of humankind.

In the last half hour of the show, Uncle Nimlash turned the questioning over to his audience, who asked questions about what it was like to be dead ("There's no such thing as death," said Jerry Garcia, "only audiences of deadheads.") and whether Jesus' mother, Mary, was still a virgin ("My mother has seven billion grandchildren," replied Jesus. "I think it's time to find a new adjective to describe her.").

At the end of the hour, Uncle Nimlash took his best shot and said to Jesus, "This hour has gone by so quickly. Will you come back and visit this show again soon?"

Perhaps it was an oversight that I hadn't anticipated this question, but even I was surprised by Jesus' answer, "Uncle Nimlash, I'd be happy to come on your program again ... but only on two conditions. The first one is that I don't have to sing again—"

Which brought a huge laugh.

"And my second condition is that I'd want Eve to come on the show with me."

The audience cheered wildly at this.

"You heard it from the Man, himself," said Uncle Nimlash. "And to all my faithful viewers today, if you want Adam and Eve to appear on this show together, go to our website and tell Eve you want her to come here."

Uncle Nimlash put his arm on Jesus' shoulders and turned to his audience again.

"Let me say, as I say at the end of every show, but now with more understanding of what it means, "God bless you all … and try to make each other happy."

The band started playing the closing theme music.

The mikes went off, the lights came down, and I saw production credits rolling on the studio monitors.

A little later, I buttonholed Jesus in the Green Room to ask him why he wanted to come back on the show with Lucifer.

He paused for a long moment then said gently, "Don't worry about things you can't do anything about, Duj."

I decided not to press him on the point. "You look tired," I told him.

He nodded, but smiled. "Know any place on this planet where a god can get a decent beer?"

Chapter Twenty-Two

"What do you do for fun?" I asked Jesus, as we were eating bangers and mashed, and drinking pints of stout, at a pub in Oxford called the Eagle and Child.

C.S. Lewis had recommended the "Bird and Baby" to us as a nice homey place where we wouldn't be bothered but he said he wasn't joining us because he already had dinner plans of his own with Ayn Rand. Personally I think Jack Lewis would have ditched Ayn in a heartbeat to join Jesus for dinner but he picked up that Jesus wasn't looking for a party.

"Is this for the campaign, or off the record?" Jesus asked me.

"Well, I'm just asking because *I'm* interested, if that's what you mean. But if you're asking me to keep what you say in confidence, of course I will." I smiled. "I won't even quote you as 'a usually reliable source.'"

That got me a smile. "You're going to have a hard time reconciling this with my public image," said Jesus.

"Look at the last few months I've had," I said, "Whatever you tell me, it's not going to be more of a shock than what I've been through already."

"I do stand-up comedy," said Jesus.

"Except for that," I said. "Is this something you're known for in Heaven?"

He shook his head. "I use a stage name and a wear a body mask."

"Have you played earth?"

"Not stand-up. This is only my third time back on earth since my execution," Jesus said.

"I can understand that," I said. "Some planet nails me up on a cross, I wouldn't want to spend my vacation time there, either."

He grinned widely. "You should do stand-up; you'd be good at it."

I shook my head. "I like what I do now. What are you into? Political humor? Observational comedy? Improv? Or something really bizarre, like Andy Kaufman?"

"I'm more in the vein of George Carlin or Steven Wright," Jesus said. "You know, a little highbrow but with some verbal pratfalls. Philosophical stuff. Seeing if I can tell a story that starts out very mundane and just let it get more outrageous, more irreverent, and more surprising until people are laughing so hard they're turning colors."

"Wow. I'd love to catch your act sometime. Where do you appear?"

Jesus looked secretly amused. "Well, there was a little club called Divine Comedy in the SoHo district of Heaven where I'd been a regular on Saturday nights for a few years now. It got burned out in the attack on the palace and it looks like I'm going to have to find a new venue."

"Anything else?"

"My act? Sometimes I'm a piano man."

"I thought you didn't sing in public."

"Not singing, just keys. It's in a classical vein, with a lot of influence from the late romantics—Chopin, Tchaikovsky, Rachmaninoff ... with maybe a little PDQ

Bach- or Victor Borge-type gags thrown in occasion-
ally."

That's when I realized I'd already seen Jesus perform his comedy act. I decided against letting him
know that I knew.

"You stick pretty much to earth-human activities?"
I asked. "You're not into galactic golf, playing dice with
the universe?"

"My father's top god in our house," Jesus said. "And
he's a pretty hard act to follow. Oh, I've played around
with some of my dad's universe-building software —
did you know that Jack and Tollers invited me to col-
laborate with each of them in their universes based
on Narnia and Middle Earth? — and one of these days
I'm sure I'll get an idea of my own that I think is worth
building a universe around. You know, Duj, I worship
my father as much as anyone else, when it comes right
down to it … and it's intimidating. I look at his cre-
ations and my tongue hits the floor. I think, 'How am
I ever going to come up with something as good as
that?'"

"You're sounding like the classic son of an over-
achieving father," I said. "You see this sort of thing
with the kids of movie stars all the time."

"Which makes me, I guess, into the classic under-
achiever. But compared to my father I'm still pretty
young and I have all of eternity ahead of me. I just
don't feel motivated to make the big move and build
my own universe yet. I'm sure I'll get over myself and
try it some day, though."

"What about your social life?" I asked. You seeing
anyone special?"

"I have some close female friends, but that's all it is," he said. "I'm actually pretty shy about women. In a lot of ways I'm pretty much a loner, when it comes down to it."

I didn't think he was telling me the full story but I didn't press him on it.

He looked at his watch.

"Listen, Duj, would you feel offended if I popped out on my own? I just realized I have a promise I made to someone that I'm going to be late for if I don't leave soon."

"So you do have other plans for the evening," I said, smiling.

"I don't date earth women any more," he said, grinning. "No, actually, I promised the Pope I'd take him deep-sea fishing in the Philippine basin at the crack of dawn and the sun will be coming up soon."

He stood up and started to reach for his wallet, but I grabbed the check before he could. "You saved me. Your money's no good with me."

"I'll let you get away with that this time," he said. "But next time it's mine. No arguments."

We shook hands. Jesus said, "I'm going to head into the men's room and translocate from there so I don't make a scene."

"I've really enjoyed getting a chance to know you better, Jesus," I said. "There's so much about you that we earthborn just don't know about you."

"That's because most people don't want to know," he said.

Chapter Twenty-Three

Jesus' words were prophetic.

"We're behind Eve four percent in the polls," Heinlein told us at our morning staff meeting on Friday the 14th.

"How close is that to the margin of error?" I asked.

"Not close at all," said Heinlein. "I like mathematical precision so my thought is that if we're going to make decisions based on polling data at all, it needs to be a large enough sampling to be useful. The margin of error in the polls we're using is one tenth of one percent."

"Do we know why?" I asked.

"Yes," Heinlein said. "We did a focus group."

"I don't need a focus group to know what the problem is," said Dr. King.

"You go first, then," I said to King.

"I don't know any other way to put this. Jesus is just too human."

"That's what came out in the focus group, too," said Heinlein. "We're soft in what should be our Christian strongholds."

"We're behind in the polls because the Savior of humankind is too human?" I asked, astonished.

Dr. King nodded. "You weren't raised a Christian so perhaps you don't have a natural feeling for this. Jesus is a mysterious, mythic figure to Christians. He's the all-wise teacher who speaks to us only in parables and riddles. He is lofty and above it all. He's called the son of God but is treated more like a stern father figure. He's morally perfect and incapable of error. The only human quality Christians are apparently willing to ascribe to Jesus is his ability to suffer pain and one brief moment of fear.

"Now, Jesus returns to earth, and Christians are confused. Jesus admits to us that he has made mistakes, particularly the catastrophic mistake that caused the very fall of our race. He gains points for his classiness in being up front about his fallibility ... more points for his willingness to make up for it on the cross ... but the Lord and Savior's shown us a side of himself that we didn't expect. We knew he was a god who became human, but we didn't expect him to be *this* human."

"The singing on TV didn't help," said Golda Meir. "That sort of show-business flashiness was beneath him."

"I thought the way he sang was gorgeous," said Marilyn Monroe.

"It was a bromide," Ayn Rand said, "overly sentimental. It sounded to me like a cross between two other bromides, *We Are The World* and *Imagine*."

"Well," I said, "the recording is getting more downloads from the Internet than any other song in history."

"Wonderful," said Meir. "Jesus can have a career as a recording artist after the Anorexics take control of this planet and turn it into hell."

"Why doesn't Lucifer have this image problem?" I asked. "She's as much at fault in the events that led to the fall as Jesus."

"It's that we had already thought of her as fallen, as one of us," said Mencken. "We had no expectation that Eve would be perfect in the first place. All the stories about her show her as a girl who liked to have a good time, right from the start. So when she comes here and looks sweet and pretty, that's all we expect from her."

"Great," I said. "We're losing this election to sexism and lowered expectations."

"We have to go negative," said Meir. "Tear away this innocent image that Lucifer's built for herself here. Show them films of the mass extermination camps in Hell. Make people realize that she's not just Eve, she's also their great enemy, Satan."

"No," said Jesus. He had popped into the meeting so quietly that none of us had even realized he had joined us.

"But why, sir?" Mencken asked.

"My reasons are not a thing I feel compelled to discuss with any of you," Jesus said.

I felt I couldn't keep silent any longer. "Your father put me in the job of managing this campaign and told me all of his creation rides on how this election turns out. I know that you still have feelings for your ex-wife, but don't you think it's wrong of you to sacrifice your father's life's work because of your own personal feelings?"

Jesus immediately looked wounded and I was sorry I had spoken up in front of anyone else.

Jesus paused a moment then said, "Don't you understand that Lucifer was the worst of my victims? That what she has become is my fault? That it was my gross insubordination to my father, my failure to use my better judgment, that began the disappointment that put her on the path to believing in nothing?"

Came the dawn and I suddenly understood. "You didn't come back to save the earth at all," I said. "You came here to save *her*. You've never gotten over her. You're just like your father, betting the house on a long shot."

"You make very free with me," said Jesus. You go too far."

"So I'm too damned arrogant to know my place," I said. "But I'm not exaggerating the truth, am I?"

Jesus howled in pain.

I felt horrible, the worst I'd ever felt about anything in my life.

He stood there for a moment like a deer caught in headlights, and spoke with his head bowed. "Everybody thinks I'm so forgiving. How could I not forgive people their sins? Without the empathy I gained from committing the biggest sin in history, I would have continued being a callous fool forever."

Then Jesus raised his head, looked directly at me and said, "Save your home world. I'll do anything you tell me."

He disappeared from the room.

I looked around the table. Everyone was staring at me in disbelief.

I have a tendency to lean on wisecracks in moments of crisis, but this time, George Bernard Shaw beat me to it.

"All too human," he said.

So I'd finally found out for what purpose I was cre-

ated by God. I was here in loco parentis to Jesus because God couldn't be here, to stand in the shoes of
the father whose job it was to tell the sweetest son in
all the universes that there was no end to the pain he
would have to endure because of youthful high spirits.

Well, if I was going to *have* to be God, then I was
going to be God.

"We're going for broke," I told the Central Committee. "There is no way I am going to make Jesus have
to decide between his love for us and his love for his
ex-wife. We will not campaign negative against her."

"Then you may have just thrown away the whole
universe," said Golda Meir.

I got mad. "You're the smartest people God ever created," I shouted. "Think of something!"

I snapped my fingers and translocated myself in-
stantly from Mount Shasta to my living room 600 miles
away.

Until that moment I hadn't even known how to do
it.

Chapter Twenty-Four

They thought of something.

"We have to *what*?" I exclaimed, a couple of hours later, when they called me back to Mt. Shasta. I was no longer going to fly for routine travel now that I'd figured out how to translocate myself.

"We have to help Jesus develop a strategy to win his ex-wife back," said General Patton.

"Dear God in Heaven," I said.

"Not anymore, unless we're successful," said George Bernard Shaw.

"He's only been trying for a couple hundred millennia or so," I said. "What makes you think that we can pull this off where he failed?"

"Because we have to," said Thomas Jefferson.

"There must still be a love connection between them," said Marilyn Monroe. "After all, neither of them ever remarried."

"Suddenly this war is turning into yet another re-make of *The Parent Trap*," I said. "Well, what do you suggest we do? Lock them both in a room with Dr. Phil? Or put Satan in psychotherapy like in Jeremy Leven's book?"

"I had something a bit more devilish in mind," said C.S. Lewis.

"Something with a plot twist," said Ayn Rand.

On Monday, October 17ᵗʰ, two weeks before the election, Jesus Christ was missing in action. We had cancelled all his public appearances, all his scheduled interviews.

It was in all the papers.

When we had made the decision on Friday to remove our candidate from public view, we were sure we would lose additional numbers, perhaps as much as another five percentage points. We thought it would look as if he was afraid or had lost interest in the election, or worse: that he was hiding because he was humiliated by his poll numbers.

It just goes to show. Human beings, especially voters, are fundamentally unpredictable. I guess that quantum unpredictability is the best proof there is of free will.

Dr. King had gotten it precisely correct. Christians wanted their Savior to be mysterious and aloof. They were used to praying to him. It was disconcerting to them when he answered their prayers.

These new poll numbers weren't at all a problem for the strategy that C.S. Lewis and Ayn Rand had cooked up together. Serendipitously, it made the strategy even more perfect.

By the following Monday, October 24th, just one week before the election, Jesus was up seven points over Lucifer. The Anorexic Party was desperate and was calling loudly for a public debate to be simulcast on live TV and satellite radio, the Internet, and in dreamland. The League of Women Voters had already sent over proposed guidelines.

I hung tough and refused to commit. We took an overnight hit of two percentage points because of it, but our overall numbers were still holding steady with a solid five percent lead.

At the end of my radio show on Tuesday, October 25th, I got another phone call from Manchu Ellins. "We need to get together," he told me.

"Will I be getting anything out of the meeting that I want?" I asked him.

"Is there anything I have that you want?"

I considered the thought that he was offering me a roll in the hay with his wife, but didn't think she would go along with it, even for her political party. I answered, "I've always wanted a ride in a McLaren F1."

"How about five tomorrow morning?" he suggested. "I have some friends at Edwards Air Force Base who let me use the old shuttle landing strip to take her up to 225 miles an hour."

"Sounds like fun," I said.

"I'll drive over and pick you up in back of your town home."

"God, no," I told him. "You can't drive around our complex without going over sixteen speed bumps. No matter whatever else there is between us, I'm not going to put the suspension of an eight-hundred-thousand-dollar car through that. I'll be waiting just inside our front gate."

This time I hung up first.

He was as good as his word and the next morning his black McLaren three-seater was parked along the curb inside our gate by the time I walked along the palm-tree lined path to the front. Caulinn Helms was not with him.

The door swung up and Ellins jumped out. We shook hands cordially and I said, "No offense, but I'm not climbing in until you let me peep you."

"I'm just a mortal man," said Ellins. "What could I do even to inconvenience you?"

"If you've studied the way I think you have," I said, "you know that even mortals can wield great power."

"Go ahead," said Ellins. "I'm here under a truce flag anyway. I've got nothing to hide."

I looked into his soul, his past and what I could see of his future, and what I saw surprised me. He was just a few weeks away from splitting up with Caulinn Helms, who was much more of a fanatic than he was, because he just couldn't handle not being touched during their sex play any more.

I didn't tell him any of that but said, "You've got a good heart and many virtues but your picture of how things work is askew. With a couple of hours conversation, if you were self-honest, I could likely convince you to switch to our side. I'm surprised Lucifer even trusts you."

Ellins looked at me strangely. "Are you under the impression that Lucifer and others of our party have your power to see inside human souls?"

I was startled. It had never even occurred to me that they couldn't, and the subject had never come up in our own committee meetings, not even security briefings. Apparently everyone was assuming their chairman already knew.

I smiled sheepishly. "I'm new at this god stuff," I admitted, hoping that opening myself up a little wouldn't bite me in the ass later. "Come on, I'm anxious to feel what this baby can do."

Ellins helped secure me into the passenger seat,

then got in himself and pulled the car out onto Hannum, turning right. He turned left onto Playa, took the entrance to the I-405 north, and in a few minutes we were cruising in the number one lane past Westwood and not long after that on the I-5 north.

We reached Highway 14 north in less than fifteen minutes, then he flicked on his radar detector and cruised along in fairly empty lanes at around 100 miles an hour. The way this car handled, if felt like we were going 30. We were at Edwards in just about an hour.

Being a movie star has its advantages. His name was on a guest list and we were waved onto the base with no problem.

I've never been one for roller coasters or other thrill rides, but this car was almost as much fun as flying! We did full-speed runs back and forth on the desert flats until the fuel gauge read low enough that unless I wanted to perform the miracle of turning water into gas, it was time to head back.

But we didn't head back. I could see a lone figure off in the distance, standing out on the desert flats.

Ellins headed toward it and well before mortal eyes could resolve the image I could see that it was Lucifer.

Chapter Twenty-Five

Manchu Ellins pulled the McLaren up close to Lucifer and popped open the door. "I believe this is your stop," Ellins said.

I was unnerved, but not enough to forget my manners. After I climbed out, I extended my hand and we shook. "Thanks, this was a blast," I said.

"My pleasure," he said, then pulled the door down and sped off, leaving Lucifer and me alone in the desert.

There she stood, one leg slightly forward, in a skimpy black cocktail dress, black high-heel pumps, and dark sunglasses over full lips. She looked sexy as hell, reminding me of Nicole Kidman in *Practical Magic* or Sharon Stone in *Basic Instinct*. It took me a moment to remember how dried up she'd chosen to look at her rally in Heaven, and to remember that there was an unbridgeable age difference between us.

"Duj Pepperman," I said, sticking my hand out to her jauntily. "Is this the part where you take me up to a high place and offer me rulership of earth if only I sell out to you?"

She laughed and shook my hand firmly. "I have the worst press agents in the universe," she said. "Don't believe everything you read."

I looked around the desert and enjoyed the cool morning breeze. I'd been out here back when the NASA space shuttles were still flying and remembered how hot it could get by 10:00 AM.

"Nice place you have here," I said to Lucifer.

"I've always loved the desert," she said. "It's peaceful. Private. A good place to think. Come on. Walk with me."

She took off the pumps and tossed them away, choosing to walk barefooted. I wondered if she had several thousand more pairs in a closet somewhere.

She walked energetically but not aimlessly; I kept up alongside her. When it became clear that she wasn't going to begin talking, I did. "What's on your mind?" I asked her.

"You get right to the point," she said. "Don't you ever just take a moment?"

"Pardon me but cut the crap," I said. "You didn't bring me out here for a romantic walk on the beach together."

"No, I didn't," she said. She stopped and looked at me. "We've never even met before. Why do you hate me so much?"

"I don't hate you," I said. "But with everything in my body and soul I despise what you stand for. I read your book so I know how wrong you got it. And by the way, you're a terrific writer. You should spend your time writing novels instead of trying to muck up other people's lives, particularly those of people I love."

"I loved him too, once," she said.

"Come on, you're a smart lady," I said. "What are you accomplishing with this rebellion of yours? It's not bringing you or any of your followers happiness; you've made joy your enemy."

"Is that what you think of us?"

"That's what I think of *you*," I said.

"And you thought I brought you to the desert to tempt you," she said.

"Is there anything that can tempt *you* anymore, Lucifer?" I asked her, pointedly not calling her Satan.

"You're a little boy, born yesterday," she said. "What sort of bribe can you possibly offer me?"

"What children can always offer their parents," I told her. "Fresh eyes to see the world around them."

She stopped, took off her sunglasses revealing large, green eyes with long lashes, and looked at me as if she was seeing me for the first time.

"I've been underestimating you," she said. "I thought you were just a cheap spin off. I can see God spent considerable time working on you."

"If that's a genuine compliment, thank you," I said. "But flattery's not going to get you around me. I'm as committed an ideologue as you are."

"I'm not an ideologue," she said. "I'm just an angel who found out the hard way that the god who created me is a liar."

"So what?" I said. "I don't happen to agree with you but so what if he is? All of this is because you found out your parents aren't perfect? All of this because your childhood friend and high-school sweetheart got his armor a little tarnished? And you call *me* a child?"

"How did you get to be so glib?" she asked.

"I'm on the radio twenty hours a week," I replied, "fielding callers who think just like you."

I stopped walking and she stopped, too.

"Can I try something?" I asked. "A little magic trick I've been practicing?"

She looked surprised, but smiled warmly. "Knock

yourself out," she said.

"Okay," I said, "I've never tried this before without going through a menu, so forgive me if it doesn't work the first time."

I waved my hands and a full-length mirror appeared in the desert, floating in mid air in front of us.

"Not bad," she said.

I let the compliment slide; I had created the mirror for a rhetorical purpose.

"Look at yourself," I told her. "You're magnificent. This is what you looked like when you and Jesus put on bodies for the first time in Eden. You're a flower in full bloom, one of God's most glorious creatures."

She looked away and made the mirror disappear.

"I was a young angel then who knew nothing of what creation meant," she said. "I had no idea how terrible being a material girl could be."

"Cute," I said. "Has it never crossed your mind that all you have ever focused on is what you *don't* want, what you *don't* like, and never on what you *do*?"

"You don't understand me at all," she said. "You think of me as some sort of powerful demon, when the truth is that I'm a lost soul who's addicted like everyone else to a powerful drug. I keep trying to go back to being a free spirit the way I started out—trying to pull out of flesh, trying to deny its hold on me — but the sensual temptations are always too much for me and before I know it, here I am again, snorting air up my nose."

"Is that what you think life is? Just a drug?"

"Yes, that's exactly what I think God's invention of life was," Lucifer said. "Creation was television. A comic book. A movie. A dream. Life was created as a thrill ride meant to hide from you the awful reality that existence has *no ultimate meaning*. Even God never found a reason behind his own existence; he just *is* and never *questioned* the fact. And when the spirits he spun off started becoming aware of the banality and meaninglessness of existence, too, God started inventing all these crazy games and toys to keep us from crying our new eyes out."

"But don't you *see*?" I said to her, grabbing her by the hands. "The meaning of existence isn't something you *look* for, as if it's a prize in a box of Cracker Jack. Meaning is where you *start*. You say to yourself, 'So here I am. Looks like I'm going to be here forever, doesn't it? Now what am I going to do with eternity? Make something beautiful that gives me joy, and find out what other exciting things others are making, or just sit around feeling sorry for myself, when something doesn't work out right, until I'm counting the grains of sand in the desert and letting myself go crazy?'"

I was on a roll and finally had her attention.

I continued:

"People born here on earth for the first time call important questions 'life or death.' But they haven't yet learned what those words mean. They think life is having a heartbeat and death is being in a coma forever. But eternal life is pursuit of joyful surprise and the only alternative, when forever is before you, is becoming the *death* of the party. You, yourself, just told me you discovered that the nature of real existence is that it's something you can't choose. It just is what it is. Isn't the *only* choice we have—the first choice we have to make before making any other choices—just how we're going to *look* at it?"

"Are all radio-talk-show hosts such deep philosophers?" Lucifer asked.

"They are if they want to stay on the air in the L.A. market," I said. "But as much as I like to hear myself talk, I don't think that's why you brought me here."

She nodded in acknowledgement. "I need a debate. Jesus asked me to appear with him on Uncle Nimlash. I propose we agree to each other's requests and we do a debate on Uncle Nimlash."

Bingo!

"This Friday, October 28th, noon local time," I said. "No flying or magic tricks, just the two of you answering questions prepared by Uncle Nimlash and his studio audience. Everything checks out as Kosher before Jesus sets foot in the studio. These are my terms. Does the devil have a deal with me or not?"

"She does," Lucifer said.

"We can skip the signing in blood," I said.

I snapped my fingers and disappeared in a puff of smoke.

I was getting really good at this.

Chapter Twenty-Six

Later that day when I had a chance to talk with Thomas Jefferson privately I asked him, "Can Lucifer or any of her followers see the divine heart?"

"They see only the outer soul," he said. "The armor they put up to hide their own true selves blinds them to the true selves of others and is their Achilles' heel. Unlike all but the most evil people on earth, who walk around celestially naked, the guilt-ridden habitually hide their true selves from those who can see them. That was why after their disobedience Adam and Eve felt so naked before God in the Garden of Eden. They did not know how to hide from him what they had done. Demanding a look at their true face is the only real enforcement clause we have in any treaty with the Anorexics. If they didn't know that *we* can know when they're lying, even to themselves, eternal evil would always be one step ahead of eternal good, the way mortals are tricked by frauds on earth."

"Then if we can see them but they can't see us, why do they trust us to keep our word?"

"Because we always have. The testament to one's honor from an enemy is its most glorious praise. But it is also why they fear and loathe us. Our ability to see them allows them to feel the pain of their own guilt. We diagnose their pain just by being honest, and that's why they must hide from us if they wish to remain ill."

"I didn't try to undress Lucifer during our meeting—

I'm not very self-confident yet and was afraid of the corruption I might see—but I don't think Lucifer was trying to hide from me," I told him.

"Then we have hope," King Solomon said.

"Europe will just be starting to go to bed when *Uncle Nimlash* begins," said General Patton. "The Middle East and Asia will already be asleep. For those who don't stay up to watch us on CNN, we're going to have to pick up a lot of audience on the live dreamcast and delayed plays."

"How are people reacting to the new phenomenon of common dreaming?" I asked the round table.

Robert A. Heinlein answered. "Our surveys and focus groups showed that some people were initially frightened when they awoke to find out other people were having the same dreams they were," he said. "But real-time morph checks show few instances of nightmarish fugues caused by the dreamscape experience itself. The dreams are only being broadcast on the REM Network so most people are just waking up refreshed."

"Excellent," I said. "Ladies and gentlemen, can you do without me chairing tomorrow morning's meetings? I've been pretty much cooped up in this fortress since the campaign began, and I'm worried about losing touch with how the voters are feeling, just as we're pulling into the home stretch." I turned back to Heinlein. "Can you take the gavel while I'm gone?"

"President Jefferson is Chairman Pro-Tem," said Heinlein.

I looked across the table to Jefferson. We locked eyes and he smiled back at me.

"President Jefferson will be my traveling companion," I told him.

A few hours later Thomas and I were sitting at a bistro on the left bank, enjoying buttered croissants and cups of *café au lait*. He had abandoned the nineteenth century garb he preferred to wear at our committee meetings in favor of a Giorgio Armani suit.

"The French are ... well, the *French*," he said. "They haven't changed in thousands of years. Did Jesus tell you that he spent a lot of his 'missing' years in Gaul?"

I shook my head and told a white half-lie. "We've been so busy talking shop that his personal life never came up."

"The French have always loved Jesus," Jefferson said, "although after getting razzed about their affection for Jerry Lewis, you're not likely to find a Frenchman who admits sentiment about anyone. Did you study *la langue française* when you were mortal?"

"*Un très petit peu*," I said, sipping my coffee. "I studied French in high school just enough to be able ask for directions to the Rodin Museum on my one previous trip to Paris. They say the French are rude to Americans but that's only because they're insulted we no longer treat French as, well, the *lingua franca*. The Parisians showed this American beautiful manners, although some of them thought at first I was German because no American could possibly go to the trouble of learning their language."

Jefferson chuckled. "I asked you about your French for a specific reason. Say in French for me, if you please, the phrase 'I am.'"

"*Je suis*," I said.

He waited.

"I'm not getting your point," I said.

"Perhaps it would help if you wrote it out," he said, handing me a pen.

I wrote "*Je suis*" on a placemat but was still drawing a blank.

Jefferson reached across the table and drew the proofreader's semicircular underline mark for making two words into one. That's when I saw it and my jaw dropped. "Jesus. I Am. The French knew his divinity before he'd even started preaching!"

"It was buried in their language as a prophecy," explained Jefferson, "so they would recognize the savior when he came to live among them."

"You know," I said, "When I was mortal I'd always thought that when you were mortal you were an atheist, like me."

"I was a gnostic, a student of the arcane," said Jefferson, "just one of many who misread old documents about Jesus having fathered a 'holy bloodline' on earth to mean that he'd survived the crucifixion and went on to get married and sire children. I didn't realize that the documents were referring to the children Jesus had fathered with Eve when he was Adam. The big secret is that the sainted blood—the 'holy grail,' in a coded pun — goes all the way back to Eden. By today's date you'd be hard pressed to find a human being that doesn't share in it."

"Then *all* the human race is royal?"

"Jesus was the ultimate Democrat," said Jefferson, who'd just finished his coffee. He spoke to the "*grande duchesse*" who had just served us. *"Madame, une autre tasse de café au lait, s'il vous plaît?'*

Chapter Twenty-Seven

Two of the nicest features of the *corpus novus* are that you don't have to sleep unless you feel like it and that you never suffer from jetlag.

Thomas Jefferson *née* King Solomon spent the next 24 or so hours giving me the grand tour of earth. We flew when we felt like seeing the view and translocated directly when we didn't. It was wonderful not having to worry about immunizations, passports, visa stamps, customs declarations, border crossings, driver's licenses, tolls, gasoline taxes, or the bone-wearying ordeal that has strangled commercial aviation. You don't fully appreciate how much crap paranoid bureaucrats have loaded onto the simple act of traveling until you don't have to put up with it anymore.

King Solomon and I stopped off in Jerusalem and prayed at the Western Wall clothed as Orthodox Jews, then King Suliman and I kept our long beards and donned traditional Islamic dress, to pray in the Al Aqsa Mosque.

From there we popped into the Chicken Ranch in Pahrump, Nevada, and spent a pleasant hour at the bar drinking with the ladies.

We spent a day sightseeing around his old stomping grounds in Virginia and Washington D.C. Jefferson gave me a personal tour of Monticello, and pointed out to me punctuation errors in the Bill of Rights when we visited the National Archives.

When we took the White House tour, Jefferson complained about how the White House had been turned from what had been intended as "a pleasant office building for the chief executive with a bedroom above the shop" into a fortress more suitable for a Caesar.

"It's my own fault, too," said Jefferson, as we were talking near his own memorial in Washington D.C. "I was so intent on expanding out west when I served as president that I forgot my natural mistrust of governmental power."

I hesitated because I knew what I was going to ask next was a sensitive topic. "How could you, who wrote the phrase 'all men are created equal,' have held slaves?"

"I could fall back on the legal argument I used at the time, that Virginia law forbade me to free my slaves." He paused a moment. "This was never recorded in scripture, Duj, but when God first told the Ten Commandments to the Israelites, the Sixth Commandment he told them was, 'You shall not murder nor shall you keep man or woman in bondage.'"

"What happened?"

"You have to understand the times. The Israelites were only a few generations separated out from people who still ate the people they conquered. Slavery existed among every people on earth at the time, including the Israelites. They were convinced that freeing their slaves would be disastrous to their way of life, and make them the laughing stock of the world. They begged Moses to go back to God and ask him to take out the slavery prohibition entirely. Moses did, and they came up with a compromise. The anti-slavery clause was moved from the commandments—their constitution, so to speak—into their regular legislations, and modified so that it merely required slaves to be freed after seven years service, if they wished to leave. I've long thought that God made a mistake by backing down, but ruling the Israelites was like herding cats—as I well know from personal experience—so likely God had no real choice about it after all."

He paused a moment. "An interesting historical note, but I evaded your question, didn't I?"

I smiled.

"The truth is, Duj, that in the mid-to-late eighteenth century I was struggling with what I saw as 'the African question,' myself. I didn't see how people dragged to the New World so terribly could ever forgive white men so I thought the only solution was to put them back on boats to Africa. In my racialist views about Africans I was not all that different from the Nazis, though I thank the Lord I was spared from contemplating a 'final solution.' But we came damnably close to a final solution for the Indians, didn't we? At least they had guns and could shoot back at us as we harried and cheated them into primitive ghettos. It's the only salve to my guilt that I have."

With his mention of guns, I decided to bring up one of my pet peeves to him: the way the Second Amendment had been interpreted by the NRA to grant an individual right to keep and bear arms.

Jefferson looked at me surprised. "You are a gun owner yourself?"

"Sure, I have a gun in my bedroom, for protection. That doesn't mean I think every yahoo should be walk-

ing around strapped like it was the Wild West. I have
no objection to unenlightened mortals being subjected
to some reasonable gun controls."

He paused a moment and I sensed there was so
much he wanted to say that he didn't know where to
begin.

"How long would it take you," he asked, "if you decided that the planet Jupiter was unsightly and you
wanted to blast it from the solar system?"

"About five minutes," I said. "I've never done anything that big before so I'd have to go through the pro-
cedure menu by menu."

"So after a five-minute waiting period," Jefferson
asked, "you can arm yourself well enough to destroy
our largest planetary neighbor?"

I could see where he was going. "I think you're
making my point for me," I said. "Jesus doesn't resur-
rect people whom his 'background check' doesn't
show can be trusted with that sort of power. And as I
understand it, some people have to go through a waiting period of centuries before they're ready for that
sort of responsibility."

"If earthly government were as unbiased and fairly
applied as the divine judgment, I would agree with
you entirely," Jefferson said. "I was in France when
the Bill of Rights was being written or I might have
suggested an even less ambiguous wording for the
Second Amendment, to make its protection of the individual right to keep and bear arms even stronger.
As it stands, I agree completely with the NRA's interpretation."

I looked startled.

"You see, Duj," Jefferson went on, "in the absence of a divine and just king, there is no mortal who can be counted on to execute the judgments of power justly and even-handedly. When I was president even I, who thought I believed in the innate equality of men, fell into the old habit of the aristocrat, thinking that because of my gentle breeding and fine education I could better decide for others what was good for them. And in my racial views I was barely short of thinking like a Nazi, for God's sake!

"But at least I understood that the foundations of a free country had to rest on a man's right to defend himself both from highwayman and tyrant, and to do that he had to be able to have enough power for this right to mean something in the real world. The more the politicians of your era distrust the common people with arms, the more they are telling the common people that they who are there only to serve them have become worthy of being feared as tyrants, themselves.

"The right to defend life from those who would abuse or destroy it is the most basic of all rights that came about as the consequence of God's creation of individual souls. As sensible-seeming laws as requiring a background check, or training prior to purchase, or even penalizing what some new aristocrat deems unsafe storage of arms has within it the assumption that rights originate not with the people but with the flip of an aristocrat's wrist, and are therefore merely a privilege to be withdrawn as the aristocrat deems prudent. Nor, I must say, is there much honest debate in this city anymore about what are the actual costs of disarming the people, when by doing so criminals are protected from instant reprisal and terrorists are given a government-guaranteed promise that they will not be opposed by anyone as well-armed as they are.

"The only solution we were able to come up with of how to have a government of imperfect men was to leave the most important powers in the hands of the people themselves, as armed neighbors and jurors, then to disperse the remaining powers the people were entrusting to government as widely as possible.

"Nowhere has our failure been more evident than in this city we designed, where soldiers under direct orders of the undivinely elected have the most powerful weapons at their disposal, yet the citizen whom they are sworn to serve is deprived of his ability to walk the streets with a sidearm appropriate to defending the lives of his loved ones and countrymen. My successors in office will, like me, live to experience the grief of their mistrusting the people with their own lives and property. I only can pray that they will not torture themselves for centuries over their fearful miscalculation as I have."

Chapter Twenty-Eight

Friday, October 28th, 12:00 PM in Television City, Los Angeles.

In addition to the normal TV cameras in the studio, there were, for the first time in earth broadcasting history, the pick-ups that would turn the present events into a dream that could be broadcast to sleepers around the world, to be translated into symbols they could grasp whether or not they were familiar with the language or cultural matrix of the actual event.

The director was counting down, "eight … seven … six … five … four …" then counted the last three numbers with his fingers, silently, and cued Uncle Nimlash who was standing center stage– no brassy theme song introducing him this time.

"Good afternoon, Ladies and Gentleman," Uncle Nimlash began, "and welcome to what I believe will be an historic event about which I can't possibly exaggerate its importance. Today on your *Uncle Nimlash Show* we will be hosting a debate between the two candidates who are running for the position of celestial governor of the planet earth.

"Neither of the candidates has seen any of the questions my staff has prepared with suggestions that have been pouring into our website, not only from you the viewing audience but also from journalists throughout the world. In the second half of today's debate, my studio audience will be free to ask questions of the candidates, and none of these questions are being prescreened. We have done our best to keep partisans of the two candidates out of our audience.

"The format of the debate is going to be simple. The candidate receiving the question will have one minute to answer, and the opposition candidate will have one minute to reply. The candidates have declined an opening statement to allow more time for questions, but they may make a closing statement if there's time left over and they have accumulated a balance of time.

"The debate is going to be fairly informal but I will do my best, with the help of my producer, who will be watching the lengths of the candidates' responses, to divide the time between the two candidates equitably. We had a coin toss before the program to determine which candidate would get the first question. The candidate of the Party of God won the toss but has elected to allow his opponent from the Anorexic Party to take the first question.

"We have asked our studio audience to refrain from applause or any other demonstrations until the conclusion of the debate.

"And now, the candidate for governor of the Anorexic Party, the First Lady of Earth—Eve."

Lucifer walked out wearing a smart, emerald-green Christian Dior original, reminiscent of an Oleg Cassini suit Jackie Kennedy had once worn. She shook hands with Uncle Nimlash firmly and seated herself in an armchair stage left of him, folding her lands on her lap and crossing her ankles demurely.

Uncle Nimlash continued:

"The candidate for governor from the Party of God, originally known to us as Adam, the first man, and later as the savior of the human race, Jesus Christ."

Jesus came out in smartly creased white slacks and a long-sleeve white silk shirt, a white silk tie, and a white silk jacket over it. He looked like a doctor, or at least a doctor on *General Hospital*. He also shook hands with Uncle Nimlash firmly, shook hands with Lucifer, and seated himself in the armchair stage right of him, leaning forward slightly with his legs about a foot apart and his hands resting on his knees. It gave the impression that he was alert but not overly nervous.

"The first question for Eve," said Uncle Nimlash. "Many observers of this election have noted that it appears to be not about substantive political issues but merely a custody dispute between a divorced couple. Would you care to respond?"

"Of course," said Eve. "I simply don't think it's true. Jesus and I have deeply felt differences on a number of important issues. He is opposed to a woman's right to choose to have an abortion; I favor that freedom. He is for a laissez-faire economy, while I believe the excesses of big business must be curbed. He would wish to do away with the current treaty that limits the size of celestial interventions into the affairs of earth, while I believe that the treaty preserves the independence of earth from outside interference. I could give you many more examples but I'm hoping to reserve some time for a closing statement."

"Very good," said Uncle Nimlash. "Jesus, you have one minute to respond if you'd care to."

"I have no response at this time," Jesus said.

"Then we will go directly to the next question, which

is to you, Jesus. It has been debated elsewhere many times during these last three weeks whether the accounts in Genesis have properly apportioned the accountability between you and Eve regarding the sequence of events that led to the fall of nature and the fall of man. Would you care to give us your perspective on this question."

"Yes, I'm very happy to take that question," said Jesus. "Eve would not have even been capable of causing such a catastrophe. It is not in her nature. I take complete and solo responsibility for causing the fall of nature and the fall of man, with all the consequent pain and suffering that followed through human history and that exists to this day."

"Eve," said Uncle Nimlash, "you have one minute to respond."

I could see that Eve looked perplexed. She had evidently come here prepared to challenge Jesus on his failings but he was pre-empting that possibility by taking responsibility for them. If she concurred with him she would come across as a bitch; but she could only dispute Jesus by admitting her own part in the fall, something she had never done, even to herself.

Which left Jesus getting the points for that question, no matter what she did.

"I have no response at this time," she said.

Uncle Nimlash looked surprised and smiled. "I can see we will be getting through more questions than I anticipated," he said.

"To you, Eve," he continued. "While it is traditional in American politics not to ask candidates questions of religious faith, this is a worldwide election covering many different peoples of widely differing beliefs. While we would anticipate a prefabricated politically correct response embracing the beliefs of all peoples, could you please tell us of your own religious background and faith, if any."

Zing! Uncle Nimlash's staff had just put a shot right across Eve's bow, foreclosing the option of her prevaricating on the question.

I wondered whether she was going to do the debate equivalent of taking the fifth.

"I regard myself as a Christian," Lucifer said. "I have witnessed for myself the historical truths that Jews, Christians, and Muslims base their faiths on. These are not questions of faith for me but inescapable reality. I would not be here if I had not been created by God and resurrected by Jesus. Any other differences aside, it would be childish of me not to be grateful."

Classy answer, I thought, and wondered for a moment, having heard quite a different speech from Lucifer in a celestial Hyde Park, whether my talk to her had some impact, or whether this was simply a political ploy.

"Jesus, would you care to respond?"

"Eve's gratitude to my father is right and proper," he said, "but there is no balance of gratitude she owes me. She has given me far more than I was ever able to give her."

Uncle Nimlash took off his glasses for a moment and looked at Jesus. "May I break format and make a comment that is not on my prepared questions?"

"If Eve has no objection," said Jesus.

Eve nodded her consent.

"Perhaps we can set aside some of these questions, Jesus, if I can anticipate some of your answers from the ones you've already given. May I conclude at this point that you have no intention of disputing Eve on any substantive issue in this debate?"

"Uncle Nimlash, that is precisely my intention."

We knew what the next question had to be. In fact, we were counting on it.

"Jesus, are you then telling us that you believe Eve is better qualified than you to govern earth?"

"May I go beyond the one-minute limit to respond to that question?" Jesus asked.

"Eve?" Uncle Nimlash asked.

"Yes," said Eve.

Jesus turned his chair away from facing the audience and faced Lucifer directly.

Here was the moment we had planned for. Jesus' answer was going to take all of God's creation and put it squarely in the lap of Lucifer.

"Eve," Jesus said, "I love you. I have always loved you. I have never loved another living spirit as much as I love you."

Jesus paused a moment and I could hear a stir in the audience.

Uncle Nimlash waved his audience into silence.

Lucifer looked stunned.

Jesus continued:

"I died on the cross for *you*," Jesus said. "I had no other god before you. It was the thought of you that gave me the courage and the strength to face the crucifixion."

I could see tears starting to well up in Jesus' eyes,

as he poured out his heart to her.

Lucifer did not look away from Jesus' gaze but I could not read her reaction. Her armor was up.

"I wanted to make up for the damage I had done which had ruined your faith in my father, in me, and in your joy of creation. When you would not stay on earth with me, earth lost its flavor for me. Do you wonder why I haven't been back here more than a few times? It's that everything on earth reminds me of your beauty and your joyful innocence and of the wonderful times we had together in the beginning. The memories were just too painful for me to be here without you. Having to stay on earth without you, even now, would be a living death for me."

Jesus took a cloth handkerchief from his jacket and dabbed the tears from his eyes.

"How can I ask the people of earth to support me in this election, when I don't want to be here without you, when I can't be here for them? You obviously care for the people of this world or you would not be here. I am withdrawing my candidacy and throw my support to you, Eve. You win."

Lucifer sat there and I could see her start to tremble.

Suddenly, her armor dropped and I could see directly into her divine heart.

I could see her youthful innocence and joy in existence shine out, as her disappointment, her rage, her bitterness, all dropped away in an instant. For the first time in thousands of years, her aura could be seen.

Lucifer's aura was not visible to the television cameras but I could see it and it would be visible in the dreamcast.

Her corona was growing in size and intensity, and she was beginning to radiate an almost blinding white light.

It must have been sensed even without seeing it by some people in the studio audience, because they became restless. Uncle Nimlash waved them into silence but suddenly a woman's voice shouted out from the audience, *"Give him another chance, honey! This is one man in a trillion!"*

The audience, waiting for any sort of trigger to release their own bottled up feelings, erupted into wild cheering and applause.

I kept my gaze on Lucifer and I adjusted my eyes so I could see past her corona to her face. She was crying.

She got up from her chair, walked over to Jesus, got on her knees and put her head on his lap.

"Oh, Adam," Eve said, crying, as Jesus wrapped his hands around her and stroked her head. "Oh, my dear one," she said. "I am so *celestially* sorry."

Chapter Twenty-Nine

It's hard to explain the full impact of the changes on planet earth over the following days and weeks.

As a mortal I lived through the American tragedies that were the assassination of the Kennedy brothers and Dr. King, the murder of John Lennon, the Challenger disaster, the Holocaust at Waco and the retaliatory Oklahoma City bombing, race riots in my home town, earthquakes and torrential storms, and the sneak terrorist attacks of September 11, 2001. As Reverend Chill had correctly explained, these were catastrophes that cause immense grief but there were also happy eucatastrophes of equal magnitude.

Put the emotional power resulting from all these catastrophes together within a period of a few days and you begin to calculate the eucatastrophic joy that was the opening day of the Gateway Arch in St. Louis as earth's first public transit station to New Heaven.

Gone forever is the mortal Halloween's ghoulish disinformation about decay and annihilation as millions of the resurrected stream back through the tunnels for reunions with their mortal loved ones and friends back on earth.

Gone is the pain, suffering, and fear of dying, as still-mortal friends and relatives are given round-trip tickets for their astral bodies to accompany departing souls through the tunnels, while ministering angels gently guide voyagers out of their discarded flesh at a freely selected moment of expiration.

Resurrection parties are now bigger deals than weddings and bar mitzvah's put together. In case you're looking for a good investment, the catering business in New Heaven is a boom industry. And while still-mortal guests really can't leaving their old bodies behind for more than a few hours at a time, most do take the tour of the Celestial Palace before catching the tunnel home.

Gone are earthquakes, tropical storms, and the necessity for airport security as people who refuse to be peeped by other passengers are now politely informed they just aren't welcome, and guardian angels monitor tectonic plates, moderate weather, and fly escort to airliners in flight.

Gone is the planetary feeling of being orphaned, as we learn of our full genealogies with the click of a mouse, and gone are silly arguments about history as kindergartener and doctoral candidate alike can go on the Internet and find links to the Tree of Knowledge's store of downloadable books, movies, and musical compositions lost for ages—and we can even send email to the original artists and participants.

Yes, there are parental controls in place on the Tree of Knowledge. Some things you have to get in your own sweet time when you're ready for them. But the amount of new information available to the human race is enough to take several lifetimes to absorb, anyway, enough to quench the thirst of the driest scholar.

Gone is tyranny and grinding poverty as even the poorest soul in the darkest dungeon can pray for liberation and find a powerful ally in his cause.

Most important, gone is the Berlin Wall separating God and his children on earth, as the inventor of all is once again welcome to take a stroll with his wife through their own back yard.

Of course you already knew all this, didn't you?

Okay.

I've been telling you this story for enough hours that I hope you've developed some affection for me, personally, and I hope you won't be bored when I bring you up to date on my personal story.

There was a big royal ceremony at the Celestial Palace where all of us who worked on the campaign lined up like at the end of *Star Wars*, and the Trinity handed out medals, with our favorite piece of music playing while we walked up to the throne and lined up.

I'm leaving the radio business. I just got hired as a talk-show host for a new telepresence network that Rupert Murdoch and Bill Gates are founding.

You should see the "A" list for future interviews in my Rolodex now.

I'm now engaged to both Estella and Sophia. There's no law against it and to answer anything else you have to say about it: it's none of your business.

A lot of the members of the Party of God have decided to buy houses on earth. I've stayed in close touch with everyone I worked with on the campaign, and even Manchu Ellins has turned out to be a good buddy. George Bernard Shaw bought a town home just a few doors away from mine, and the dinner parties we've been invited to at his house have been legendary.

Elvis is back in the building.

Old Blue Eyes is back in town.

O.J. and Nicole are back together.

Children now live in a nation where they are not judged by the color of their skin but by the content of their character.

The Rams are back in the City of the Angels, where they belong.

And my daughter, Felony, has signed Robert Zemeckis to direct the movie version of this book.

Not for nothing have we returned this planet to its original name.

Eden.

Chapter Thirty

Because the electoral contest for the governorship of earth was called off before the balloting began, I never found out how it would have turned out. We only know it would have been a tight race. The Neilson polls we conducted during the debate showed Jesus ahead, but the polling was within the margin of error so that doesn't tell us anything definitive.

If you get a chance, could you cut out the ballot card at the end of this book, mark your vote, and mail it to the preprinted address? You can either cast it as a secret ballot or you can fill in your name, address, and age if you want your vote to be on record.

If you check off the "I want to be on your mailing list" box, I'll be able to get in touch with any of you who are interested in ever getting together with each other for meetings or a convention.

Or, you can go to my website at http://www.dujpepperman.com, and cast your ballot there.

If you're under eighteen, please do not give us any information without the permission of a parent or guardian.

You know, people think that Heaven is a place. It isn't really. The beautiful buildings, the nice parks, the good restaurants that I found when I first got to Heaven, all that is just stuff. It's good stuff, stuff that makes life more comfortable, more convenient, and more fun, but when all is said and done, as George

Carlin puts it, it's all just stuff.

That's why it was no big deal for God to abandon Heaven to Lucifer. As soon as she'd agreed to God's one condition for surrender, that any resurrected humans and angels who wished to stay with him were free to leave, he had back all of Heaven that mattered.

God never surrendered anything of lasting value to Satan. All that she'd got was leftovers. And when her heart finally melted and she saw the truth, Lucifer realized that not only had she been fighting for nothing, she had finally achieved it in full measure.

Our race is used to suffering the losses of wars. Some of us cry about the stuff we lose. I'm as guilty of that as the next guy. But there is no real disaster except the loss of someone you love, and in the universes that God has made, the only way you can lose someone for good is if one of you goes into hiding, yourself.

I got a postcard from Jesus and Lucifer just as the two of them left New Heaven for their honeymoon. They never got a chance to have one the first time they were married. Believe it or not, they're spending their honeymoon in Hell.

Jesus suggested a plan to Lucy that they both incarnate themselves into her universe, propagate a new genetic line, and introduce some revolutionary individualistic ideas into that dismally uniform world, saving the billions of identical people that Lucy had unintentionally condemned to misery.

I can't wait to find out how it went. I'm sure it would be a story worth telling.

This has been

Written in Culver City, California.
Completed October 1, 2001

About J. Neil Schulman

J. Neil Schulman is the author of two Prometheus award-winning novels, *Alongside Night* and *The Rainbow Cadenza*, short fiction, nonfiction, and screenwritings, including the CBS *Twilight Zone* episode "Profile in Silver."

His first nonfiction book was *Stopping Power: Why 70 Million Americans Own Guns*, of which Charlton Heston said, "Mr. Schulman's book is the most cogent explanation of the gun issue I have yet read."

Schulman's next book, *Self Control Not Gun Control*, was his *magnum opus* on personal, political and spiritual power.

He has been published in the *Los Angeles Times* and other national newspapers, as well as *National Review, New Libertarian, Reason, Liberty,* and other magazines. His books have been praised by Nobel laureate Milton Friedman, Anthony Burgess, Robert A. Heinlein, Colin Wilson, Walter Williams, and many other prominent individuals.

Schulman is a popular speaker on a variety of topics, and a frequent radio-talk-show guest. In 1992 he hosted and produced his own weekly radio program, broadcast on KPRO AM, Riverside, California. He was on ABC's *World News Tonight* as an expert on defensive use of firearms during the 1992 Los Angeles riots, and in 1999 was interviewed twice on the Fox News Network for the fifth anniversary of the Brown-Goldman murders, regarding his alternative theories about the crime.

J. Neil Schulman is a pioneer in electronic publishing, having founded in 1987 the first of two companies to distribute books by bestselling authors for download. He is currently developing the Julius Schulman Center for the Living Arts in Pahrump, Nevada, as a teaching and performing arts center. His personal web site is at http://jneil.tv/ and his edress is jneil@pulpless.com.

Instructions

Mark the box for the candidate of your choice. Any information you supply below the ballot is optional and will not affect your vote.

After cutting along the dashed line to detach ballot page, fold in half, top to bottom. Tape or staple bottom. Make sure address is visible. Place stamp on address side and mail.

You can also fill out this form at
http://www.dujpepperman.com,
and cast your ballot electronically.

CELESTIAL GOVERNOR OF EARTH
FIRST DISTRICT, MILKY WAY GALAXY, MATERIAL CONTINUUM

Mark box for no more than one candidate	*Anorexic Party* **EVE** Earth Mother	**1**➡️ ☐
	Party of God **JESUS CHRIST/ADAM** Saviour	**2**➡️ ☐

END OF BALLOT

Name _____

Address _____

_____

eMail_____

Age _____

If you're under eighteen, please do not give us any information without the permission of a parent or guardian.

_____
If Under 18, Name of Parent or Guardian

_____
Parent or Guardian's Signature

☐ I want to be on your mailing list for notices of any author appearances, bookstore signings, conferences or conventions related to the topics in this book.

cut along this line

PLACE
FIRST-
CLASS
STAMP
HERE

Duj Pepperman
150 S. Hwy 160, Suite C-8
#234
Pahrump, NV 89048

www.ingramcontent.com/pod-product-compliance
Lightning Source LLC
Chambersburg PA
CBHW030516020726
47494CB00004B/1121